PRAISE FOR MARK ELDISH

Gary Fenton's Second Chance is the funniest thing I've read all day, and it's almost time for elevenses.

— HIS PUBLICIST

Maybe now he'll stop with the lame 'I'm writing' excuses and help me around the house a bit more.

— HIS WIFE

I don't mind God being a woman, but did he really have to make her swear like that?

— HIS MOTHER

I fear that he might well go to hell for this.

— HIS LOCAL VICAR

I'll make damn sure he does.

— DORAN SALT

GARY FENTON'S SECOND CHANCE

MARK ELDISH

DOMINUS PUBLISHING

For my family, with love.

CHAPTER ONE

Life is a pain in the arse.

Pain, especially when it's in the arse, is a very shitty thing.

I have therefore concluded that life itself is a very shitty thing.

And that's why I've decided to end mine.

Tonight.

Of course, when I say that life is a very shitty thing, I'm speaking in general terms. There are, I admit, a few brief sparks of joy to be found in even the most miserable life. Watching the England football team play their way to a World Cup semi-final is one such spark. So is being invited to a discreet Friday-night lock-in by the landlord of some cosy little pub. Or receiving a first class blow job from a woman who excels at the fine art of fellatio thanks to natural instinct, and not simply because she's handled more wood than a lumberjack.

But, brief sparks of joy aside, I maintain that life is nothing more than a big ball of crap that's been rolled up, dried out and thrown at you with great force from a modest distance. If you manage to avoid it's impact, that's fine. Good on you. Well done, mate. Have a cigar. But if the bugger smacks you square in the side of the head and you end up resenting the fact, then you aren't to blame. Not the way I see it, anyway.

That Buddha bloke clearly shared my point of view, because he astutely observed that, 'All life is suffering.' (Yeah, I know, it's amazing what you can learn from some of the magazines that people leave piled up in the dentist's waiting room.) In a similar vein, King Solomon supposedly said that, 'Everything is meaningless.' (Sunday school, in case you were wondering.) So, I know for a fact that I'm not the only person who ever felt this way. There are at least three of us, and probably quite a few more.

Now, before you start getting the wrong idea, let me tell you that I'm not the kind of person who you might normally expect to have suicidal tendencies. I'm not crack-addicted, pain-inflicted or deeply depressed. I'm just a normal, extremely average guy who has become totally and utterly bored with his life.

I've lost the will to live. It's as simple as that.

For the record, my name is Gary Fenton. I'm thirty-five years old and I live alone in a small flat in the crappy part of Brighton. The place is a wreck, but because I get paid sod all to work my bollocks off in a local DIY superstore, and I have no other career prospects, there's nothing I can do about that. As for relationships, well... there haven't been any since I was in my late twenties, when I was jilted by a girl called Vicky, who I thought was my soul mate but turned out to be a lesbian. I've had a few one-night stands since then, but nothing that's gone further than an awkward conversation over coffee and Corn Flakes the next morning.

As I said, life is a pain in the arse, and it's a very shitty thing.

I wouldn't have any problem with life if it were something sensible, like an electric toaster. When you buy a toaster from the store, you take it home, unpack it, plug it in and insert a couple of slices of bread. A few minutes later, you pretty much know whether or not it works as you expected. If it produces two slices of piping-hot, golden-brown toast, all well and good. But if it burns your bread to buggery, you take it back and ask for a refund.

Unfortunately, life isn't sensible, like a toaster, because if your life screws up, you're pretty much stuck with it.

Or at least, that's what I used to think. I used to think that I had no choice but to suck it up and keep going. To grin and bear it, keep a stiff upper lip, and all that.

But then, the thought hit me:

Why?

Why should I have to live a very shitty life if I don't want to? We all die, eventually, so why not just bring the inevitable event forward by a few decades and put myself out of my misery?

The more I thought about this solution, as radical as it was, the more it made sense. And, believe me, I did think about it very carefully. I might be pissed off with life, but I'm not stupid, so I analysed the situation carefully, weighing up the pros and cons of both living and dying. I even calculated how many self-inflicted orgasms I could possibly be missing out on. The answer to that question was 7,280, and it was calculated on the basis of four tugs per week—I'm habitual, but not compulsive—multiplied by fifty-two weeks per year for another thirty-five years. That sounds like a lot, but having established the rather unadventurous habit of relying on only three basic masturbatory fantasies, two of which I adopted in my teenage years, I decided that suicide was still the way to go.

In case you're thinking that I'm suffering from a *grass is always greener* complex, and looking forward to some kind of Utopian afterlife, I'm not. I don't believe in an afterlife. In fact, I don't believe in anything. To me—and I think Richard Dawkins would be more than happy to back me up here—it seems perfectly clear that all of the stories we hear about God, karma, heaven, hell and similar imponderables are pure bollocks. They're fairy tales, and the only reason they exist is to help alleviate the fears of the feeble-minded, who can't accept the painful and obvious truth that their meaningless lives will eventually come to an unavoidable and permanent end.

I have no problem facing such harsh realities. I know that, one day, my misery will end and that will be that. But, whereas most people say that you never know when your time will be up, I beg to differ. If you're willing to end your own life, you can choose your own time. And I have chosen tonight. Superstitious people would be proud of me, because it's Friday the thirteenth.

I started walking my final walk towards Brighton Pier at just after seven o'clock in the evening. The sky was mostly clear, there was a comfortable July breeze and the streets were still busy with locals and tourists alike. Under the red and yellow lights of the pier entrance, boisterous teenage lads stood in small groups, loitering with intent to get some hot sex action from any of the similarly sized groups of giggling teenage girls who were also hanging around. Parents were taking their kids to get ice cream and candy floss from one of the stalls situated at the beginning of the walkway. Young lovers held hands and whispered sweet lies to one another as they strolled through their own rose-tinted version of the scene. The air was thick with the stench of hot dogs and hamburgers.

I realised something new as I observed all of this. Namely, that all of our waking hours are spent trying to escape from reality in some way. We work our nuts off all week long, Monday to Friday, so that each weekend we can afford to watch movies, play video games, listen to music, drink too much and do whatever else might temporarily distract ourselves from ourselves. We like to put the banality of the working week behind us and pretend to be people we are not: People with a sense of purpose in their lives.

If we take away all that we do to try and escape from the drab reality of existence, then the drab reality is all that we have left. We eat, sleep, work and fuck (if we're lucky) day after day after day after day after day after day. And for what?

For nothing.

King Solomon really was a wise old bloke.

Everything is meaningless.

There are many possible ways of committing suicide. You

can take an overdose, put a gun to your head, hang your-self from a favourite tree, jump in front of a train, slit your wrists, take a hot bath with a hair dryer... the choices are potentially endless. Unfortunately, all of the options that I have just listed require a certain amount of courage, and since courage is not something that I have in vast quantities—or even in paltry quantities, for that matter—I have decided on a slightly less dramatic exit from this life.

I will be jumping from the pier.

Jumping from the pier has a number of benefits as far as I am concerned. First, it requires no complicated set-up, since I happen to live in a town which has a perfectly good pier for jumping purposes. Second, it will be impossible for me to bail out and change my mind once the jump has been made—an important advantage, given my aforementioned lack of courage. Third, it is guaranteed to be effective, for the simple reason that I am one of those people who never learned to swim, so I couldn't possibly stay afloat for much longer than a few minutes, even if I wanted to.

One thing that hadn't occurred to me about jumping from Brighton Pier was the fact that attempting to do so on a busy Friday night in the middle of summer was bound to attract unwanted attention. I had made my way towards the quietest location as casually as I knew how, but as soon as I climbed over the white painted railings and onto the narrow ledge on the other side, a small but annoying group of teenagers gathered around me.

'You're not gonna jump are ya, Mister?'

The voice belonged to a freckle-faced redhead who seemed to be leading the throng. She stood in a pair of burgundy-coloured Dr. Martens boots and folded her arms accusingly. The left side of her head was shaved close to showcase an ear full of piercings.

My first response to her question was to avoid responding to it. Instead, I tried the time-tested trick of ignoring her in the hope that she'd get bored and go on her merry way, much like fundamentalist street-preachers tend to do whenever they're confronted with rational arguments against their beliefs. Unfortunately, the ruse proved entirely ineffective.

'Hey, Mister,' she said. 'Are you deaf or somfin'?'

I glared at her, annoyed by her flippant bastardisation of the English language, but she only seemed pleased that I'd acknowledged her presence.

'I said, you're not gonna jump, are ya?' She asked the question with a raised voice, mouthing her words in an exaggerated manner, presumably so that I might be able to lip read if I actually were deaf.

I forced a polite smile. 'Yes, that's exactly what I'm going to do,' I said. 'So, if you don't mind, I'd appreciate a little privacy.'

'Fuckin' hell mate, don't do that. Don't top yerself!'

These words had been uttered by a scrawny young skinhead in torn blue jeans. He was dragging hard on a cigarette.

'Why not?' I pointed to the slow-burning cylinder in his mouth. 'You're doing exactly the same. My way is quicker, that's all.'

He looked at me uncomfortably for a moment, then

tossed the offending item to the floor and snubbed it out with the sole of his boot.

'Things are never that bad,' the redhead said.

'She's right,' the skinhead agreed. 'There's always somethin' worth livin' for.'

I grinned at their naivety, and wondered how they'd feel about life in ten years time, when it had slapped them around a bit.

'What about your parents?' the girl asked. 'Your mum and dad? What would they think?'

'They're dead.'

'Oh...' Her face flushed and she glanced awkwardly at her friends. 'I'm sorry.'

'Don't be,' I said. 'They can't feel a thing.'

'Then what about your girlfriend, mate?' asked another of the teenagers. This one had obviously been sporting a short mohawk in the recent past, but he had since changed his mind about its suitability for some reason, and now appeared to be letting it grow out.

'No girlfriend,' I said.

'Well, work then,' he persisted. 'They always say you should throw yourself into your work. You know, when you're feeling a bit down and out of sorts. It's supposed to be one of the best things you can do.'

I sighed. 'I work in a DIY store where they play the same forty-seven minutes of soulless muzak over and over again, from eight in the morning until ten at night, seven days a week. On a good day, I spend most of my eight hour shift stacking shelves. On a bad day, I have to mop up the piss that the old folk leave on the floor in the men's toilets because they're no longer steady enough on their feet to aim straight. Believe me, throwing yourself into the ocean is a lot more appealing than throwing yourself into that kind of work.'

The teenagers looked at each other. They were probably racking their brains for that one phrase, that one supremely motivational sentence, that would be powerful enough to give me pause for thought. Unsurprisingly, they found nothing.

'Look,' I said. 'As much as I appreciate you all trying to talk me out of making what you consider to be a dreadful mistake, there really isn't anything you could possibly say that would change my mind about this. Just remember that, okay?'

The freckle-faced redhead looked confused. 'Okay, but—'

'Good, then that's settled.'

With those final words uttered, I turned to face the vast expanse of the ocean and leapt forward with my arms outstretched before me. I heard a loud gasp, although whether that was from the group of teenagers or myself, I wasn't quite sure. What I did know with some certainty, as gravity eagerly pulled me down towards the undulating carpet of water below, was that my miserable life would very soon be over.

People often say that truth is stranger than fiction. It isn't. According to Hollywood, the moments before death usually involve time standing still, or everything happening in slow motion. It's all very poetic and moving, with the dying man reliving whole slices of his past in a single heartbeat. Eventually, he finds himself floating down a long tunnel towards a bright light and whatever kind of afterlife the screenwriter chooses to portray.

In reality, my death involved none of those things. I hit the water. Hard. Painfully hard. But apart from that, the whole dying process was about as uneventful as my life had been. The cold water grabbed at my body and I struggled for a while as the natural instinct to survive overcame my conscious desire to end it all, but exhaustion soon prevailed and the ocean won the battle quite effortlessly. I recall a sense of profound silence as the water dragged me down into its deep, murky darkness, and everything went black.

CHAPTER TWO

'Killing yourself was a bad idea, my friend. A very bad idea, indeed…'

There are two things that surprised me when I regained consciousness. The first was the fact that I had regained consciousness at all. (Shouldn't I be dead already? And didn't dead people tend to stay that way?) The second was that I found myself staring up at an Indian bloke who was grinning down at me with wide eyes. The intensity of his gaze made him appear borderline crazy, and I'm only saying borderline out of politeness.

I sat up quickly and looked around, trying to get my bearings. I was in a cell of some sort. The walls, floor and ceiling all seemed to be fashioned from grey-coloured stone, and were pretty much identical apart from a bare metal door with no handle that was set into the wall directly in front of me. The only things inside this cold, sterile cube, in addition to the crazy guy and myself, were two bunk beds set against opposite walls. The bunks were hard, and my body ached in protest at having slept on one of them for what felt like far too long.

The Indian guy was still looking down at me with his wide eyes and his mad grin. He was wearing grey jogging bottoms and a matching T-shirt. The front of the shirt had the word SINNER stamped across it in bright red capital letters. At first, I thought that it must have been the name of his favourite band, or maybe of a lesser-known Marvel Comics character that I hadn't yet discovered, but then I looked down at myself and saw that I was wearing the exact same outfit, including the exact same shirt.

'Where am I?' I asked. 'How long have I been here? And what the hell am I wearing?'

I motioned for him to move out of the way as I swung my legs off the bunk and planted my feet on the floor. That's when I saw that I was wearing a pair of mule slippers in the very same shade of grey as the rest of my ensemble.

'And who the hell are you, anyway?'

'My name is Amit,' he said. 'Amit Patel.' He padded across the cell and sat down on his own bunk. 'And although I am very pleased to be making your acquaintance, I must say that you have left it far too late to start asking so many questions.'

'And why is that, exactly?'

'Because the damage has already been done,' he said, wagging his finger at me for emphasis. 'You have committed the most heinous of sins, and now it is time for you to pay for your grievous misdeed.'

Grievous misdeed? Most heinous of sins?

'Is this a mental institution?' I asked. 'Are you officially insane? Is that it?'

He thought about the question for a moment, and then shrugged. 'Perhaps we are both insane, in a way. But this is a place of punishment, not one of protection.'

Amit's response was vague to say the least, so I looked around again to try and piece the clues together for myself. Cold, bare walls. Hard bunks. A door with no handle. Matching uniforms. 'Is this a prison cell?'

'Yes, I suppose it is, of a sort.'

'But why? What have I done?'

He pulled his head back and raised his eyebrows, as if suddenly surprised by my simple enquiry. 'You do not remember committing the most heinous of sins?'

'Well, it would help if I knew what that was.'

'It was killing yourself, of course!'

I rubbed my forehead, maybe in the hope that I might be able to massage away my growing sense of confusion. 'Of course I remember trying to kill myself,' I said. 'But I don't understand why I ended up in prison for it. I mean, it's not like I succeeded or anything. Having to carry on living should be enough of a punishment, surely?'

Amit laughed. It wasn't a polite chuckle or a casual snigger, but a long, loud belly laugh, as if he'd just heard the funniest thing that it was ever possible to hear. 'You are too naive, my friend,' he said when he'd finally calmed down. He wiped a tear of mirth from the corner of his eye. 'You are here precisely because you *did* succeed! You are dead, right now, even as we speak!'

There are moments in life when somebody says something that seems to make time stand still, and no matter how long you struggle to get your head around it, you can't bring yourself to respond in any meaningful way.

This was one of those moments.

As if sensing my dilemma, Amit shook the humour from his face and leaned forward with a more serious expression, his elbows resting on his knees, his hands clasped together. 'My friend, this is a holding cell in the afterlife. All suicidal souls must come to a place like this in order to await their judgement. When you have received your judgement then you will be reborn in a manner befitting your crime.'

'Reborn? You mean reincarnation?'

He nodded solemnly.

'But that's absurd,' I said.

Amit shrugged. 'Perhaps it is, but it also happens to be the truth. By committing suicide, both you and I are guilty of the worst possible sin, and so we must now pay the price by being reborn as a lower form of life.'

'Like what?'

'That is not for me to say. Some traditions teach that we will return as insects—perhaps as a humble maggot or dung beetle. Others insist that even those creatures are too lofty for suicidal souls such as ourselves, and that we will instead be born as even lesser life forms, such as pubic lice or genital warts.'

'That's just gross.'

'Potentially, yes,' he said. 'But at least I would have a fifty-fifty chance of getting close to some pussy next time around.' He leaned back and slapped his thigh, delighting in the apparent genius of his own joke.

I took the pause in our conversation as an opportunity to reflect on the bizarre situation that I found myself in.

The last thing that I remembered was jumping from Brighton Pier, hitting the water and taking in a lungful of the salty stuff. After that, everything had gone black.

Logically, that should have been the end of it. My heart should have stopped beating, my brain should have died of oxygen starvation and my lifeless body should have been swept ashore a few days later to be discovered by an innocent passer-by—probably an old man walking his dog on the beach at some ungodly hour in the early morning. But no. Instead of all that, I had woken up in a strange cell and my only companion was a deranged Indian guy who was now telling me that I could well end up being reborn as either Jock Itch or Fanny Fungus. You can call me a party-pooper if you want to, but neither option struck me as being particularly attractive.

Think, I told myself. You're a rational human being, and you know that this kind of thing just doesn't happen. It isn't possible. So how come you're experiencing it? What's the most sensible explanation you can come up with?

I sat on my bunk for several minutes, pondering the latter question and scouring my brain for a possible answer to it. When it finally hit me, I jumped to my feet and looked over at a rather startled Amit.

'It's a dream,' I said. 'You, me, this cell... it's all a dream.'

He smiled and then shook his head. 'It is not a dream, my friend. You merely want it to be a dream so that you can dismiss the reality of the present moment in order to preserve your preconceived notions of the afterlife.'

It sounded like a well-reasoned argument, so I responded with an equally well-reasoned retort. 'Bollocks,' I said. 'I know it's a dream, and I can prove it.'

His left eyebrow arched like a caterpillar with sudden stomach cramps. 'And how can you do that, exactly?'

I walked over to his bunk and motioned for him to get to his feet. Reluctantly, he did so.

'Now, hit me,' I said.

'What?'

'Hit me.'

'For what reason? You have done nothing to harm me.'

'I know that.'

'Then why should I hit you? That would not be a very nice thing for me to do.'

'It's nothing personal,' I said. 'It's just an experiment. If this is all a dream, which I can assure you it is, then I won't feel a thing. I'll simply wake up. Probably on a beach somewhere with a dog licking seaweed off my face, if my theory is correct.'

'And if your theory is incorrect?'

'Don't worry about that. Just give me your best shot and if I don't wake up we can discuss it later, can't we?'

He looked at me carefully for a long moment, then shrugged and turned to walk back towards his bunk. I was about to protest when he span back around and quickly snapped his fist into my face. His general manner had been of a fairly unassuming bloke, all meek and mild, but my God, he could punch. It felt like he had hit me with a mallet. The pain was real, and so was the blood dripping from my nose.

'Jesus, Amit!' I blotted my injured face on my forearm, leaving a messy smear of red. 'You could have given me a bit of warning first and let me brace myself.'

The Indian smiled as he walked over to his bunk and sat down. 'For what purpose?' he asked. 'If this really was a dream, you would not need to brace yourself for my strike.' He pointed at the blood on my arm. 'We have reached an interesting conclusion to this experiment, don't you think?'

If the truth be told, I didn't know what to think. Even the concept of thinking was beginning to seem redundant. It was becoming increasingly apparent that I was an atheist in some kind of afterlife—a stranger in a strange land. This wasn't something that my rational mind was particularly keen on accepting, but as Sherlock Holmes once said to Dr. Watson, 'When you have eliminated the impossible, whatever remains, however improbable, must be the truth.' I wasn't quite at that stage just yet—there was still an obstinate part of my nature which was convinced that I would soon wake up and discover that this whole episode was nothing more than a delusion of one kind or another—but the idea that I really might be experiencing a different kind of reality was beginning to find a home in some dark corner of my consciousness.

I walked over to my half of the cell and reclined on the vacant bunk, my hands clasped behind my head. I made out that I was staring at the ceiling, but I was really casting a series of discreet glances at Amit and trying to figure him out. After several minutes of getting absolutely nowhere, I decided that it would probably be a good idea to take a more direct approach. 'So, how come you seem to know what's going on here?' I asked, and as soon as those words had escaped my mouth, the answer dawned on me. It was an answer so tremendously obvious that I sat upright with a huge grin of realisation. 'You're a stooge, aren't you?'

He furrowed his brow. 'A stooge? What do you mean?'

I stood up and walked over to the door, examining it carefully. 'This is some kind of wind-up, that's what I mean.'

The puzzled look remained on his face.

'I mean it's a joke,' I said. 'A gag. A prank. You found me on the beach, dragged me to this place and tried to make me look like a fool.' I laughed at my own gullibility. 'Well, you succeeded, so can we go now?'

The door was a mystery. It was definitely forged from some kind of metal, as I'd first thought, but it wasn't any kind of metal that I'd seen before. The surface was impossibly smooth to the touch, as smooth as a mirror, and completely free from blemishes, but as a solid as cast iron. There was no obvious way of opening the thing, and I was becoming increasingly frustrated with the whole situation, so I kicked it. To my surprise, striking the door didn't make any kind of sound, but it did send a shockwave of pain through my foot. The grey mules afforded me little protection, and if I'd kicked any harder, I might well have broken a toe.

'This place is killing me,' I said, pacing back into the middle of the cell to try and walk off the pain.

Amit smiled his irritating little smile. 'You are wrong yet again, my friend. How can this place be killing you when you are already dead?' He shook his head slowly. 'You are a stubborn man, I will give you that.'

'The only thing I want you to give me is a straight answer.'

'And I have done that quite eloquently,' he said. 'This is not a dream and I am not a stooge.' He kicked off his slippers and drew his feet up onto the bunk so that he could sit cross-legged, like a yogi. 'My name is Amit Patel and I am here for the very same reason that you are. I committed suicide. The only reason I have more insight than you into what awaits us is because I have studied the writings of the gurus.'

'The gurus?' I couldn't help but grin at this. 'Which gurus?'

'It is not important, which gurus. You would simply make fun of them even if I were to tell you. What is important is that I am not surprised to be here because I know that I must be punished for my sin.'

The pain in my foot had eased to the point where I felt able to stop pacing around, so I returned to my bunk and carefully lowered myself onto it. 'But if you say that you knew about this place in advance—from your gurus, or whoever—why did you commit suicide in the first place?'

He shrugged. 'Why do any of us do the things that we do? Perhaps it was my destiny, or just a moment of madness. All I know is that, on one particular day, I felt an overwhelming urge to put my head in the oven and turn on the gas, and so I did precisely that.'

I tried to think of something suitable to say, but couldn't.

'Besides,' he continued, 'death is not so much of a very big deal when you know that it is only temporary. The really interesting question is why a non-believer such as yourself would want to end it all if he didn't really believe in an afterlife.' A smile crept onto his face again. 'Or perhaps, deep down, you really did believe. Perhaps you just didn't want to admit it.'

'You couldn't be more wrong,' I said. 'There isn't an ounce of me that ever believed in an afterlife, or in gods, spirits, angels or gurus, for that matter. The whole spirituality thing is nothing more than a crock of bullshit designed to deceive and manipulate the masses. Show me a religion, any religion, and I'll show you a ludicrous fantasy that preys on irrational fears and exploits wishful thinking.'

He parted his lips to reply to my damning statement, but was interrupted by the cell door opening abruptly. There was a man standing in the doorway. An impossibly muscular bloke wearing a white shirt, white chinos and white shoes. He had a thick silver chain hanging around his neck, like a rap star who hadn't yet sold enough records to buy a gold one, and the facial expression of someone chewing on wasps.

'Gary Fenton,' he grunted. His voice was deep, and I don't mean regular deep, but weirdly deep. Inhuman. Almost like a rumble.

'That's me,' I said, suddenly aware that my throat was dry and that my sphincter was desperately trying to curl itself into a tight ball of petrified muscle.

'Follow me,' the man said.

He turned and started walking away.

I shot a nervous look at Amit, but he seemed unperturbed.

'You had better do as the good man says,' he shrugged. 'If you keep the Powers That Be waiting, they may decide to send you back as a tape worm.'

I tried to think of a response that would satisfy my desire to be witty and clever, or at least nonchalant, but I failed miserably. All I could do was give him a feeble nod before setting out to follow the grunting man in white, leaving Amit chuckling to himself in the cell behind me.

CHAPTER THREE

The world outside the small grey cell was reminiscent of something that you might see in a big-budget science fiction movie. I followed the oversized man-thing through a complex maze of corridors, the walls of which appeared to have been carved out of some kind of pale-blue crystalline material. The ceilings and floors were constructed from white marble. Everywhere I looked, there were large blokes in the same white uniforms that the grunter ahead of me wore. Some were walking alone and some walked in pairs. Some were being followed by startled-looking individuals who were obviously in a very similar predicament to myself, and we exchanged frowning smiles of empathy as we passed each other on our way to who knew where.

I followed the grunter for several long minutes, and on a few occasions I wondered if we weren't just repeating a bizarrely circuitous route, because every corridor looked exactly the same, with several others branching off to the left and right in patterns that were pretty much identical.

Eventually, however, we turned into a corridor which broke that pattern, because it was a cul-de-sac with no exits on either side. At the end of this corridor loomed a large silver door. Grunter led me all the way up to it, then stood to one side and stopped dead.

'In there,' he said.

'Don't you say please around here?'

He flared his nostrils, and I immediately regretted my flippant tone.

'Now,' he said, and before I knew what was happening, he had opened the door and pushed me backwards into the room beyond. I opened my mouth to protest, but it was too late. The door shut in my face with a metallic thud.

'Well, well, Mr Fenton. We meet at last.'

The voice was female. I did a quick one-eighty and found myself in an expansive and rather elegant board-room, the like of which I'd seen in dozens of Hollywood films but had never encountered in real life thanks to the fact that I was neither a mover nor a shaker of any description. An extremely large boardroom table—I'd say about forty feet in length and twenty feet wide—dominated the centre of the room. About ten paces in front of me was an empty chair, and at the opposite end of the table, the owner of the voice was sitting on a large, jewel-encrusted throne.

She was a heavy black woman wearing golden dunga-rees over a maroon-coloured long-sleeved top. She also wore an expression of extreme distaste, as if I'd just brought a very bad smell into the room. Her hair had been shaved to sculpt a flat top, large gold hoops the size of fists dangled from her earlobes, and bright yellow varnish made her long fingernails look like talons resting on the surface of the table.

'I'm sorry, do I know you?' I asked, even though I was pretty damned sure that I would have remembered having seen such an imposing woman at any point prior to this.

'No,' she said, 'but unfortunately I know you, and far better than you might think.' She gestured with her chin to the empty chair in front of me. 'Sit down.'

Reluctantly, I did as she said. I'm not sure why, exactly. Maybe I felt that I didn't have much of a choice in the matter. Whatever the reason, I sat in silence and she stared at me.

And stared.

And stared some more.

'You say you know me,' I said, desperate to break the silence. 'So who are you, exactly?'

The staring continued for a moment longer, and then she shrugged. 'I have many names.'

'Just one will do.'

'Kali.'

'Interesting name,' I said.

'Does it mean anything to you?'

'No, not really.'

'Alright. Then maybe I should pick one that's more familiar to you.' She tilted her head back and looked down her nose at me. 'How about Brahma? Vishnu? Shiva? Jehovah?'

'Jehovah as in Jehovah's Witnesses?'

'Jehovah as in most Abrahamic traditions,' she said.

I smiled at the notion.

She raised her eyebrows, clearly unimpressed by my response. 'It wasn't a joke.'

'So what are you saying, exactly? That you're God?'

'Do you have a problem with that?'

'Unfortunately I do,' I said.

'And what might that be?'

'Well, I'm an atheist.'

'So?'

'So I don't actually believe in God.'

I'm not sure how, but I knew as soon as I'd uttered those words that I'd made a mistake. A big mistake. Massive. As if to confirm my remarkable sense of intuition, the sound of thunder shook the entire room and the lights flickered angrily. The woman at the other end of the table was staring me down with the eyes of a rabid dog.

'Do you really think that I give a flying fuck what you believe, Mr Fenton?'

She didn't speak the words, but rather boomed them, her voice making the thunderous sound of a moment ago seem positively affectionate by comparison.

I swallowed hard, all too aware that I'd overstepped the mark, so I didn't dare to answer her question. Instead, I shrugged awkwardly and shuffled in my seat, like a schoolboy who'd been caught prodding the girl in front of him with a pencil that he'd previously used to pick his nose. That had only happened once, you understand, but the memory of the event was as vivid as any other from that time.

The woman inhaled deeply, as if to calm herself, and the lights eventually settled down to their earlier non-flickering state. 'Ordinarily, you would have been reborn by now,' she said. 'But unfortunately, you are not an ordinary individual. Regardless of what you profess to believe about me, the afterlife, or anything else, your suicide has set in motion a catastrophic chain of events. And that, Mr Fenton, is the only reason why you have been brought before me.'

It occurred to me that all of this could still be a dream. Whilst it was true that Amit's surprisingly vicious punch to my face had caused me some pain, maybe it had only been imagined pain. I'd read somewhere that people can wake up from a dream, only to rush to work, put in a solid eight hours and then wake up in bed again to realise that they'd simply been dreaming that they'd woken up the first time. With such weird shit having been chronicled by the learned scientists who contribute on a regular basis to *Reader's Digest* magazine, it didn't seem unreasonable to assume that something similar might be happening to me right now. Maybe I was still drowning, and all of this was simply my dying brain confronting the irrational possibility that my atheistic beliefs were unfounded. If that was the case, I was more than happy to play along and see where my unconscious concerns would take me.

'What do you mean?' I asked.

She stood up and took a step back from the table, then turned and started pacing slowly, back and forth, across the far side of the room. 'Every soul granted the privilege of being born in human form has within it a seed of destiny, which is a blueprint of the purpose that it is designed to serve over the course of its incarnation. Most seeds of destiny are rather basic in nature, so a man might be born with the purpose of providing a happy and comfortable home for his family, or a woman with the purpose of loving her children and raising them to be strong, independent people in their own right.'

She returned to her throne and rested her hands on the back of it, then gave me a long, serious stare. 'Sometimes, however, the seed of destiny is more ambitious. The seed for Neil Armstrong was to set foot on the moon. The seed for Winston Churchill was to lead his country to victory over the forces of evil. The seed for Marie Curie was to develop the theory of radioactivity.'

The problem with listening to people talk is that there's no fast-forward button. I was impatient for her to get to the point, but at the same time I was cautious about airing my impatience, just in case she had a stock of lightning bolts to go with the clap of thunder that I'd heard a minute or two earlier. Learning from my previous mistake, I simply nodded my understanding and hoped that she would get a move on.

'These particular Seeds of Greatness are allotted on a random basis so that the system of destiny is fair to all.'

'Like a lottery, you mean?'

Her upper lip curled distastefully for a moment, as if she had once again whiffed my stenchy presence, but then she conceded a nod.

'I suppose it is, in a way. And, like a lottery, sometimes the most undeserving of souls happen to get lucky and win a jackpot.'

I watched her carefully as she sat down on her throne and glared at me.

'And that's where you come in,' she said.

'I'm going to win a jackpot?'

'You already did. Before you were born.'

I looked at her silently, wondering whether she was

talking about a real lottery jackpot or her metaphorical seeds of something or other, and desperately hoping that it was the former.

'Your destiny, Mr Fenton, was to play a key role in saving mankind from extinction.'

So it was the latter. Bloody typical.

'Unfortunately, you decided that your life was a little too boring for your taste, and so you chose to commit suicide. However, when you did that, you automatically set the human race on a path towards absolute and unavoidable annihilation.' She flared her nostrils. 'So, congratulations. Not only have you fucked up your own life, you have also completely fucked up the lives of everyone else.'

I didn't like where this dream was going, but there were so many loose ends to her mysterious tale of woe that I had to press on. 'I'm really not with you,' I said. 'I work in a DIY store, and a pretty crap one at that. If that was the best I could do for a career, how was I ever going to be able to save mankind from extinction?'

She shook her head. 'I don't have the time to give you those details right now,' she said. 'The only reason you are in this room is for me to tell you that you will be sent back to Earth in your current incarnation, and that you have exactly seventy-two hours to put things right. Fail in that quest and not only will the days of the human race be numbered, but I will personally ensure that you spend the rest of eternity in a state of continuous and extreme discomfort. And if you think that I was a nasty bitch in the Old Testament, lemme tell you... that was me in a good mood.'

'But what do I have to do?' I asked. 'What do you expect me to put right in just seventy-two hours?'

She put her fists on the table and pushed herself to her feet. God, like an old man with piles, just couldn't seem to sit still.

'An agent will be sent to provide you with all the information you need,' she said. 'For now, all you have to do is formally accept the task that I have set before you.'

'And if I don't?'

Thunder. Impossibly loud rumbles that shook the room and nearly knocked me off my chair.

'Okay, okay,' I said. 'I accept.'

She smiled. It wasn't a pleasant 'nice to see you' smile, but a 'got him by the balls and gonna squeeze them tight' kind of smile.

'Good,' she said. 'In that case, you can go.'

And that's when, for the second time in as many days, everything suddenly went black.

CHAPTER FOUR

The next thing I knew, a horrible jarring sound was searing into my consciousness. I have to admit that it took me a moment or two to recognise what it was, and when I finally did, I felt sure that I must be mistaken, because it sounded exactly like the ringing of a telephone. And it wasn't the sound of just any telephone, but of *my* telephone—the special Lara Croft model that I'd won several years earlier in a pub raffle, and which I had, in my weaker moments, imagined having intimate relations with as I drifted off to sleep.

I opened my eyes, and there I was, lying on my bed in my crappy little flat. It wasn't untidy, you understand. I actually managed to take care of myself pretty well, and I'm no stranger to a duster and a can of furniture polish when the need arises, but the flat itself was crappy from a structural point of view. For example, there was an ugly brown crack which ran diagonally from one corner of the bedroom ceiling to the other. I'd often wondered how it had come to be there, and why it was brown, of all colours, but now I was wondering something else entirely. Namely, how the hell did I end up back here on my own bed after everything I'd been through in the last day or so? Had it really all been nothing more than some bizarre kind of dream?

The phone rang again.

I reached over to my bedside table, lifted Lara from her cradle, my thumb tucked snugly under her ample bosom, and put her glossy red lips to my ear.

'Yeah?' I mumbled, and as I did so, I became aware that I was stark naked. The only thing that protected my modesty (should a single guy who lives alone ever need to worry about that kind of thing) was a sealed brown envelope resting on my happy stick. As if that wasn't alarming enough, when I came to move the envelope I discovered that it had been stuck in place—a tad too securely, if you ask me—with Sellotape.

'It's gone nine-thirty and you were due in an hour ago. Where the bloody hell are you?'

It was Hargreaves, my boss at Piece o' Hut, and the only person in the whole of East Sussex who failed to realise that he was running a DIY micro-chain that was in desperate need of rebranding. 'Sorry,' I lied. 'I must have overslept...'

'And for the last time, Fenton,' he snarled. 'You'll be working through your lunch breaks for the next three days to make up for this. And if you're not stacking shelves by ten, you're finished working here for good. Am I making myself clear?'

Crystal, I thought.

'Yeah, I'll be there,' I said, and I dropped Lara back

down into her cradle, wondering what she would make of all this.

Removing the envelope from the most sensitive part of my anatomy was a painful process involving a ridiculously sharp pair of nail scissors and an uncommon amount of concentration. If I'd known that this was going to be part of my post-suicide morning routine, I would have trimmed my pubes beforehand. As it was, I just had to roll with the punches and blot the resulting tears from my eyes with a Kleenex.

The envelope was postcard-sized, and had my name typed neatly on the front.

MR GARY FENTON.

As if it was an invitation or something. Except that there was no invitation inside. Just a few cryptic sentences embossed in gold capital letters on a small slip of the most luxurious pearly white paper I'd ever seen:

DEAR MR FENTON,

YOU HAVE BEEN GIVEN AN EXTREMELY RARE SECOND CHANCE.

FAILURE TO REDEEM YOURSELF WITHIN THE NEXT SEVENTY-TWO HOURS WILL RESULT IN YOUR IRREVOCABLE TERMINATION.

YOUR ASSIGNED AGENT WILL LIAISE WITH YOU AT 1400 HOURS TO PROVIDE FURTHER OPERATIONAL INFORMATION AND A LIMITED AMOUNT OF ASSISTANCE.

YOUR KEYS ARE ON THE COFFEE TABLE.

I stared at the message, my brain puzzling over questions that were too numerous to handle all at once. Did I actually drown last night, or not? Perhaps those kids at the pier fished me from the ocean? But if so, how did they manage to get me home without my knowledge? Was that whole thing with God, Amit and the afterlife really nothing more than the bizarre delusion that I had suspected it to be? More importantly, when and why had I been stripped naked? Why had someone taped an envelope to my body? And why the hell had they taped it to my Johnson, of all places?

There was no way that I was going to be able to figure out any of this in a hurry, so I had a quick shower, threw on some clothes, grabbed my keys (they were on the coffee table, as stated in the note) and made my way to work. For once, the banality of stacking shelves on a Saturday morning seemed quite appealing.

Although Hargreaves would no doubt argue the point endlessly, if you've seen one DIY store, you've seen them all, and the one that I worked in was exactly as you'd imagine it to be. This particular branch of Piece o' Hut (there were just two, nationwide, the other one being in

Eastbourne, a few miles down the coast) boasted no fewer than seventeen aisles of paints, brushes, tools, spirit levels and all the other stuff that keeps middle-aged people busy when the pubs are shut and there's nothing of interest on television.

Despite the size of the store, there were just five permanent members of staff, not including Hargreaves himself. Selfie-queens Rebecca and Kirsty were on the checkouts, model railway enthusiast Fred liked to keep himself in the warehouse, I was on perpetual shelf duty and a Sudoku addict called Kay did the admin. They were all fairly decent people, if not a little quirky, and every one of them would rather be doing something more creative with their lives, but they were all stuck in the exact same Catch-22 situation as I was. They couldn't afford to take time off work to look for alternative employment because they needed to put in as many hours as they could to pay the bills that they already had. Life, as I'm sure I've mentioned before, is a pain in the arse.

I was fortunate that Hargreaves had locked himself away in his office by the time I got to the store, because it meant that I could slope in quietly, pull myself into my fashionable lilac overalls and start working without any grief. In times of stress, stacking shelves is a surprisingly therapeutic activity. Once you know what goes where (something you learn on an intensive thirty-minute course which takes place on your very first day) you can pretty much do the job on automatic pilot.

That gives you time to think

To meditate on the important things.

Like, why the hell am I still not dead yet?

You'd think that suicide, of all things, would be something that a person should be able to get right—even a self-confessed hopeless case such as myself. You go to the pier, jump off, breathe in a good lungful of ocean and Bob's your uncle. Dead.

But no, not me. I came back. I don't know how, or why, but even my carefully planned suicide hadn't gone the way I'd intended it to.

A part of me was curious about what might happen at two o'clock. According to the note that had been so considerately adhered to my tadger, that was the hour at which my 'assigned agent' would liaise with me. But what kind of agent was the note referring to? Government? Secret? Travel? I wrestled with this question, and many more, for the entire morning, and still came no closer to reaching any firm conclusions. Then, just as I was making my way towards the back of the store for another load of boxes, a customer derailed my contemplations by stepping flamboyantly in front of my trolley.

'It never ends, does it?'

He spoke with an American accent, and judging by his impossibly white hair and the smile creases around his eyes, he was in his early fifties. He was wearing a smart white suit, white shirt, white tie and matching white leather shoes that made him look more like a tap-dancing televangelist than a typical DIY shopper.

'I'm sorry?'

'The daily grind. It never ends.' He indicated the shelves behind me, a third of which were still waiting to be filled.

'No,' I said. 'Not for me, anyway.'

'The name's Barr,' he smiled. 'Perry Barr.'

'Like the greyhound track?'

He looked non-plussed. 'What's that?'

'Don't worry,' I said, not really being in the mood for a lengthy conversation with a total stranger. 'How can I help you? Are you looking for something in particular?'

'Actually, I was looking for you.'

'Me?'

'Sure. You're Gary Fenton, right?'

'Yes...'

'So weren't you expecting me? Didn't you get a note? To expect an agent?'

I looked at my watch. It was two o'clock, on the dot.

'You're the agent?'

'I know, it surprises me too. Come on, let's go.' He grabbed my arm and started ushering me towards the store's main exit. 'We have lots of work to do, and we have to move fast.'

'Hey, no, I can't,' I said, rooting my feet to the spot and pulling my arm free. 'I don't know who you are, or what you want, but I've got more than enough work to do here, thanks.'

'Please,' he laughed. 'You hate this place.'

'Maybe I do, but I need the money.'

'Money can't help you now, pal. Come on.'

He walked outside and waited for me to follow. I turned to glance at Kirsty, who was filing her nails at Checkout 1. She had a look of boredom on her face and was chewing a pink wad of Hubba Bubba like a cow chewing its cud.

'If Hargreaves asks after me, just tell him that I had to pop out for ten minutes, yeah?'

She nodded apathetically, which was just about as

enthusiasm as she could show during working hours, so I nodded my appreciation and made my way to the exit.

'Let's walk,' Perry said when I emerged from the building.

'Okay. But I only have ten minutes and then I need to get back to work.'

He laughed, shaking his head as if I'd said something ridiculous.

'What's so funny?'

'You are.' He kicked a stone away from his path.

'Why?'

'Because you're not going back. Not now. Not in ten minutes. Not ever, maybe.'

I stopped walking and squared up to him. 'Hang on a second,' I said. 'Who the hell are you to be telling me what I will and won't be doing?'

It was at that moment that the gentle smile on his face disappeared, and he straightened his stance. I swear he must have grown a good six inches in the space of a heartbeat. Either that or I'd suddenly shrunk by the same margin.

'I'm an Agent of the Council of the Most High God,' he snarled. 'And you're in a shit-load of trouble. She sent you back for a reason, and it wasn't to stack frickin' shelves.'

He wasn't joking. He was looking at me with the kind of deranged intensity that you only usually see in the eyes of serial killers, cult leaders and fundamentalist vegans, and I didn't like it one bit.

CHAPTER FIVE

There are three rules that I always try to live by. Number one, don't let anyone tell you what to do. Ever. Number two, don't allow people to think that they can intimidate you in any way, shape or form. And number three, never follow the first two rules if you think that doing so might put your physical well-being in jeopardy.

It was my adherence to this incredibly sensible third rule that made me accept Perry Barr's invitation to discuss the 'shit-load of trouble' situation over a civilised cup of coffee. It wasn't that I thought he might actually get aggressive, you understand. I just didn't want to dig my heels in too deep and find out for sure. What I did want to find out was what these people thought I'd done and how I was supposed to put things right. Not because I intended to do anything about any of it, but simply because the events of the last eighteen hours or so had been bizarre enough to make me genuinely curious.

We walked in silence to a small coffee shop on the promenade and sat down at a window table on cheap but comfortable fifties-style bench seats. The white tables, pale blue benches and vertical stripes in the same colours on each wall gave the whole place a fresh, seaside atmosphere. Perry didn't seem to notice any of that, but simply sat in silence, looking out towards the ocean. Even when the coffees arrived, he didn't speak. He just stirred the black liquid slowly and rhythmically, as if engrossed in some weird kind of caffeine meditation.

'What exactly are you here to tell me?' I asked when I could bear the silence no longer. 'I mean, I know it's supposed to have something to do with last night, but what, exactly?'

He stopped stirring and put the white plastic teaspoon on the thick sand-brown saucer. It's funny how colours tend to be more memorable in moments of heightened tension.

'You're gonna find it hard to believe, pal.'

I waited for elaboration, but it didn't come. 'So try me.'

'Okay,' he said.

He dipped his hand into the inside pocket of his jacket and removed two photographs, then carefully set one of them down in front of me. It was a portrait shot of a woman—a brunette who was in her late twenties, by the look of things, with a clear, pale complexion, sparkling blue eyes and lips to die for.

'You like her?' he asked.

'I'd have to be dead not to,' I said. 'Who is she?'

'Her name is Natalie Kaylan. She's your soul mate. We had her scheduled to knock on your door at eight o'clock last night when her car broke down. Thing is, you were gargling the English Channel at the time, so that didn't happen.

Anyway, the idea was that you were meant to fall in love with this gal. Next year you were meant to marry her. The year after that, you were meant to have your first child together.'

Without giving me even a moment to wrap my head around what he had just said, he set the second photograph down alongside the first. This was a shot of a young guy in his late teens. He looked ordinary enough facially, but he was sporting a rather strange looking hairstyle and what appeared to be a silver lamé shirt, both of which gave him the appearance of someone who was destined to be single for a very long time.

'Who's this?' I asked.

'Jonathan Fenton,' Perry said. 'He was going to be your great grandson. He was also going to be a pretty good biochemist who discovers the only way to prevent the human race from succumbing to a devastating plague in the year 2109.'

I glanced down at the picture again. And then at the one of Natalie. And then at Perry.

The man was clearly a loon.

'Look, I'm sorry. Is there some kind of point to all of this? Because if there is, I'm not getting it.'

He shook his head and rolled his eyes towards the ceiling, as if exasperated by my admission. 'Then let me spell it out for you,' he said. 'The only person capable of preventing the complete annihilation of mankind in the next century is your great-grandson, Jonathan. But last night you committed suicide. Which means that you weren't around to meet Natalie as scheduled, so now you won't fall in love, get married or have kids. Which means...'

'That I won't have any grandchildren either. Or great-grandchildren.'

'Right,' he said. 'And if there's no Jonathan Fenton then there's no solution to the plague. End of mankind. All your fault.'

We sat in silence for what felt like several minutes, with Perry drinking his coffee and me trying to let everything sink in. It was an unbelievable story, but for some reason I wasn't inclined to dismiss it as readily as I normally would. The idea that my suicide had made me solely responsible for the eventual extinction of the human race was clearly absurd, but then a lot of absurd things had happened since my suicide attempt.

'The note I had on me this morning mentioned a second chance,' I said. 'What's that all about?'

'Simple. You have a mission.'

'A mission? To do what?'

'To find Natalie Kaylan and get her to fall in love with you under your own steam. Having read up on your background, especially concerning relationships, it's not going to be easy. But you have seventy-two hours, minus the ones you've already lived today, to make it happen.'

'Why seventy-two hours, specifically?' I asked.

'Because it's three days, and God likes threes.'

'Threes?'

'Three-dimensional space, three states of matter, three primary colours, three wise men, three persons of the trinity, three French hens. Like I said, she likes threes.'

'Fair enough,' I said, not seeing any point in pursuing the matter any further. 'So I have three days to make this girl fall in love with me.'

He nodded. 'If you pull it off, you save mankind and

get to stay here on earth with your soul mate for the rest of your natural life. You'd get a fairly decent afterlife package as well.'

'And if I fail?'

'You'll be called before the Council of the Most High and sentenced to termination.'

'Is that bad?'

'No, it's a goddamn picnic. Whaddaya think? Of course it's bad. It's worse than you could possibly imagine. But I'll get into the small print later. For now, just accept that failure isn't a viable option.'

I looked at him for a long moment, and then I asked the question that I would have asked a lot earlier if I'd had my wits about me. 'So who exactly are you? I mean, I know your name. And I know that you're an agent. But what kind of agent?'

'I'm an agent of the Council,' he said. 'That's a group of high-level angels who take care of stuff on behalf of Her Highness, and agents are people like me, who take care of stuff on behalf of the Council. I suppose, if you were religious, you might call me a low-level angel.'

'And I suppose, if I were gullible, I'd believe you,' I said.

'Well, you asked.'

'Yeah. Silly me.'

I picked up my coffee, which I realised that I hadn't yet finished, and took a sip.

'You want proof?' he asked.

The coffee was now cold, so I set the cup back down on the saucer. 'Can you provide it?'

He shrugged. 'Well, that depends on what you want.'

It was an honest answer, but it stumped me. What *did* I want? Despite the events that had led up to this moment, I still considered myself to be a fairly rational person, and so I would rather suffer a mental breakdown than have any kind of mystical experience. That being the case, what would it take for me to suddenly change my position? What proof would I need before I was ready to accept the possibility that Perry Barr was telling the truth?'

I gazed out of the window, looking for inspiration. A gull was soaring out towards the ocean, and for a moment I considered asking him to make it plummet like a stone, but I quickly decided against that idea. Not only would that be childishly cruel, but I knew that I would pass it off as a coincidence even if he were to somehow succeed. Come to think of it, I could probably come up with an explanation for almost anything which would make more sense than believing in angels.

And then I smiled. There was one thing that he could do which, if he pulled it off, might convince even me, or at least convince me enough to go along with things for a while longer.

'Okay,' I said. 'List five things about me that nobody knows.'

'Secrets, you mean?'

I nodded. 'But big secrets. Stuff that I wouldn't even think about sharing with anyone else.'

He pursed his lips as he considered my proposal, but then shrugged uncomfortably. 'I don't know about that,' he said. 'Seems kinda nosey, if you don't mind me saying...'

'You mean you can't do it?' I was enjoying his discomfort, because he was clearly trying to backtrack.

'Sure, I can do it. I just wouldn't want to embarrass you, that's all.'

'Let me worry about that,' I said.

'Seriously?'

'Absolutely. Whenever you're ready.'

I leaned back in my seat and folded my arms, waiting for him to begin. *One Mississippi. Two Mississippi. Three Mississippi.* And then, just when I was feeling confident that he'd soon rise from his seat and shuffle off to whatever institution he'd obviously escaped from, he hit me with his opening statement.

'Okay. Number One: When you jerk off, you think about your old Sunday school teacher, Miss Beecham. Not all the time, but most of the time. Now and again you like to treat yourself to a bit of variety by imagining your Lara Croft telephone coming to life and demanding that you allow her to pleasure you right there and then, and that's Number Two. Good job you didn't win a Godzilla lamp, huh?'

I laughed, but it was a nervous laugh. The bastard had nailed me. I don't know how, but he'd reached inside my head and helped himself to my two favourite masturbatory fantasies. Could anyone do that by guesswork alone? I mean, a Sunday school teacher and Lara had to be pretty common, but he'd referred to Miss Beecham by name, and somehow he knew that the Lara of my dreams had been inspired by a telephone, of all things. The odds of being that specific by chance had to be incredible.

'Number Three: Once, when you were thirteen, you stole a pair of your next door neighbour's panties from her washing line. Not only that, but you also decided to try them on. For six straight months you seriously thought that you might be some kind of sexual deviant. In actuality, you were just a horny adolescent being inquisitive.' He paused and smiled. 'And you still have those very same panties tucked away in your bottom drawer.'

It was getting hot in here. My cheeks were burning. I looked awkwardly around the cafe. The woman who had served us coffee twenty minutes ago was wiping down the counter, which I hoped was far enough away to be out of earshot. I smiled weakly when she looked in our direction, and she smiled back, thankfully oblivious to anything that Perry had said.

'Alright, can you talk about something other than sex, please?'

'Hey, it's your dirty mind that came up with this stuff, not mine.'

'Just, something else, okay?'

'Okay,' he shrugged. 'Number Four: When you were seven, you accidentally killed your pet goldfish, Rusty, by taking it out of the bowl to see how long it could hold its breath. When it stopped moving, you put it back in the bowl and went crying to your mommy, but you never admitted what you'd done. Over the next three weeks, you threw up five times because of the guilt. You thought you were going to hell because you'd committed murder.'

Bastard. Poor old Rusty. Why did he have to go and drag that one up? There was no way that all of this could be guesswork. I felt sick.

'And finally, Number Five...' He paused and leaned in close over the table. 'You didn't commit suicide last night simply because you were bored. That's what you tell yourself, isn't it? That life's a piece of shit, and all that crap? Well, you and I both know that wasn't the real reason.'

I looked at him defiantly. 'So what was it, then?'

'It was because you were scared.'

'Bollocks,' I said. 'What have I got to be scared of?'

'Trying,' he said.

I shook my head. 'Sorry, but you've really lost me this time.'

'So far, every time you've tried something, you've failed. Often miserably. So you just got scared of trying any more. If you don't try, you can't fail, right? But at the same time, you can't succeed either. So you thought, to hell with it. Better to be dead than to keep banging your head against a brick wall.'

And there it was. My life—and my attempted death—in a nutshell.

I would have hated to admit it out loud, but Perry Barr was spot on.

CHAPTER SIX

We walked back towards my flat in silence. My head was spinning with so many thoughts, memories and images that conducting any kind of conversation whilst putting one foot in front of the other would have been impossible.

Perry didn't seem to mind the lack of communication. As far as I could tell, he was occupying himself quite happily by casting admiring glances at the various women we happened to pass by on our journey. I don't know if it was the dazzling white suit that he was wearing, or the confidence that he radiated as he walked, but he got a surprisingly high number of flirtatious smiles right back from them. If I didn't have plenty of other things to worry about, I might have felt a tad jealous. After all, he was old enough to be my dad, or thereabouts, and nobody ever gave me a second glance. I was relieved when we eventually got back to the flat, and I waved him through the hall and into the lounge, still without saying a word.

'Jesus, you actually live in this place?'

'Yes, why?'

He sniffed around for a few moments. The room had definitely seen better days, but I'd kept it reasonably tidy, or so I thought. Perry didn't appear to agree. He wiped a finger across the surface of the mantelpiece, looked at his fluffy grey fingertip and immediately screwed up his face.

'The filth in here is unbelievable.'

'That's not filth. It's dust.'

'There's a difference?'

'Of course there's a difference,' I said.

He raised an eyebrow inquisitively and waited for me to elaborate.

'Well, dust is just dust,' I explained. 'But filth... well that could imply anything, from old bits of leftover pizza to spatterings of bodily fluids.'

He looked back at his finger and gagged. 'You're pretty goddamn disgusting sometimes, you know that?'

I had every intention of arguing the point, and I actually got as far as opening my mouth to respond, but as I did so there was an almighty crash in the hall. I turned quickly and saw a tall, wiry figure enter the room. Like Perry, he was elegantly dressed, but his suit was black, perfectly matching the colour of his hair and carefully manicured goatee beard. The man brushed a few splinters of wood from his lapels and forced a smile at us.

'I'm afraid I had to break the door down,' he said matter-of-factly.

'You had to do what?' I took a step to the right so that I could look into the hall. All I saw, apart from the gaping nothing where the door should have been, was a pile of broken wood on the floor. 'Christ, couldn't you have knocked?'

'He isn't the knocking type,' Perry said.

That comment took me by surprise. 'You know this guy?'

Perry nodded, but I could tell from the look in his eyes that he wasn't happy about it.

'So you haven't completely filled him in on the details,' the man in black said.

'When you're one of the details, it isn't something that I like to rush into,' Perry sniped.

The man sniffed dismissively. 'Then perhaps I should introduce myself.' He turned and gave me a polite nod of the head. 'Doran Salt, and the pleasure is all yours.'

'Doran Salt? Is that your name or a condiment?'

'It's an anagram,' Perry said, but he didn't look at me as he did so. Instead, he continued to hold his gaze on the guy in black, as if afraid of taking his eyes off the door-kicker for even a moment.

'Of what?'

'Of your worst nightmare,' Salt smiled threateningly.

I took a step back without even thinking about it. Quite why I did that, I'm not sure, but there was something about this guy that made me feel very uneasy.

'Don't worry, he can't hurt you,' Perry told me.

'Hurt him? I intend to destroy him!'

'Destroy me?' I'd known the bloke for less than two minutes, and already he was picking a fight. 'What the hell have I done?'

'You haven't done anything... yet,' Salt said. 'In fact, you atheist types are normally quite well behaved, which is a rational choice given that you believe in neither forgiveness nor redemption.'

I had no idea why he was talking about me being an atheist, or how he knew that I was one, but his mention of rationality was encouraging, because it meant that there was a chance, however slight, that I might be able to talk myself out of whatever trouble I was supposed to be in. I hadn't had much success in talking my way out of anything so far, but surely that just meant that it was time for my luck to change? Maybe, if I approached him in the right way, he would conveniently forget about any intention he had of destroying me.

'So what's the problem?' I asked as casually as I knew how.

'The problem is that the bitch in charge has elected to give you a second chance,' Salt snarled. 'I had assumed that getting you to kill yourself would be the end of the matter, but apparently I was mistaken. Even so, what's done is done, and I regret to inform you that I cannot—and I will not—allow this quest of yours to succeed.'

Perry stepped forward without hesitating. 'You can't touch him while I'm here,' he told the man in black. 'You know that.'

'I'm well aware of the rules, Mr Barr.'

'So why are you here?'

'Because I know that this... specimen...' He paused to indicate me with a disdainful wave of his hand, 'doesn't stand a chance of succeeding without you.'

Perry looked puzzled for a moment. 'So?'

Salt smiled patiently, and the look of puzzlement on Perry's face suddenly transformed into one of fear.

'You mean...?' Perry's eyes were wide.

'I'm afraid so,' Salt nodded. He walked to the hall and cupped a hand to his mouth. 'It's showtime, Vinnie,' he called.

'Oh, Jesus, no...'

Perry's voice trailed off as a tall, wide skinhead entered the hall. He was scowling like an angry pitbull, and quickly stepped over the remnants of my front door to join Salt in the middle of the lounge. He fixed his gaze on the white-suited agent, who was beginning to retreat back towards the mantelpiece, and then moved in fast to deliver a swift punch to his gut.

I winced as I watched Perry fold to the floor like a rag doll. Vinnie wasted no time in reaching down and lifting him as easily as if that really were the case, and then threw him across the room. The legs of my coffee table snapped like twigs as it broke his fall, but the guttural noise that Perry made on impact was evidence enough that it hadn't been a soft landing by any stretch of the imagination.

'Stop,' I said. Why it had taken me so long to protest, I don't know. Shock, maybe. 'Leave him alone.'

Salt laughed. It was a cold, dark laugh, the kind of which I'd honestly never heard before. It wasn't the sort of laugh that you would hear on a ghost train or even in a horror movie, but a genuinely evil sound that filled my mind with a broad range of images, including scenes of animal cruelty, human madness and a creeping sense of thick, sticky blackness.

Perry shook his head to try and retain consciousness. Blood was streaming from his nose. He made a brave attempt to get up, but a swift boot to the side of the head from Vinnie sent him reeling into the nearest wall.

'Fuck, that's enough!' I said, but nobody was listening. Vinnie took another step towards Perry and booted him again. And again. And again.

Panicking, I looked around the room for some kind of

weapon, and spotted the empty wine bottle that I'd used as a candle holder since the previous New Year's Eve. Without really thinking things through, I grabbed it and lunged for Vinnie, bringing it down hard on the back of his shaven head. Rather than collapsing, as you might have expected him to, the bastard simply turned to look at me and grinned. Then he shifted his attention back to Perry and continued dishing out his mindless punishment.

What happened next, I can't quite explain. One minute, I was watching Perry take the worst beating I'd ever seen in my life, and the next I was jumping in front of him so that Vinnie's boot would hit me instead. Except that it didn't. Instead, the steel-capped toe stopped an inch short of smashing my nose into a dozen bony pieces.

'Get out of the way, Mr Fenton,' Salt said. 'This is none of your business.'

'Of course it's my business,' I said, and it was at that moment that I realised why Vinnie's boot hadn't turned my face into a pulp. 'He said you can't touch me because it's against the rules. And the only way to get to him now is through me. So fuck off, the pair of you.'

Salt stared at me thoughtfully. 'If you would allow me to do my job, I could guarantee that you would be well rewarded. In the afterlife, I mean.'

'And how exactly would you do that?' I asked. 'No, don't tell me. I suppose you're an angel too, is that it? Like Perry?'

'Oh, I'm far more powerful than Perry.'

'Is that right?'

'Certainly,' he said. 'So what will it be? Wealth? Fame?

Power? Supersized genitalia? I could give you all of that and throw in a harem of women as a bonus, if you'd like.'

'And if I don't like?'

His eyes turned black, and I don't mean that as a figure of speech, but as a genuine physiological observation. It was as if the pupils of his eyes had expanded to swallow up the white, like hungry black holes, and now he appeared even meaner than he had when he'd first strolled into the room.

'Then you will pay,' he snarled. 'When you fail in your quest, you will pay dearly, and for a very long time.'

'Well that's okay, because I don't intend to fail.'

Salt flared his nostrils, then looked at Vinnie, who still had one boot frozen in mid-kick, and pointed to the hall. Vinnie obeyed the silent command, returned his boot to the floor and left the room. Salt watched him make his exit, then gave me another one of his hard stares before doing the same, leaving me with a badly beaten Agent of the Council to tend to.

'Is anything broken?'

Perry shook his head. 'Not unless you include your coffee table. Or my pride.'

'Well, pride's a sin anyway, right?' I quipped, and I was glad to see him manage a smile in response. 'Come on, let me help you to the sofa.'

I brushed away what remained of the table, and helped him to his feet. He was a lot steadier than I thought he might be, and he managed to walk to the sofa himself, albeit slowly.

'Thanks, I'm okay,' he said. 'Just a bit shaken, is all.' He winced as he eased himself down into a sitting position.

Satisfied that he wasn't seriously injured, I left the

room and returned a few moments later with a glass of water, a shaving mirror and a pack of antiseptic wipes. 'Thought you could use some supplies,' I said, handing them over.

'Thanks,' he nodded, then took a sip of the water. 'And thanks for helping me out there. You showed some real gumption, so I stand corrected. You're not a complete loser after all.'

He pulled one of the antiseptic wipes from the pack and set about cleaning up the blood that had already begun to dry on his face. I was relieved to see that his wounds had only appeared to be a lot worse than they really were, and that they amounted to little more than a few superficial scrapes. This was clearly a guy who could take a beating.

'That's nice to hear,' I said. 'But I couldn't just stand there and let the bastard kill you, could I?"

'That would be the least of my troubles.'

'You think?'

He responded with another nod of the head. 'You're not the only one who has a goal to achieve here. If I fail in helping you to succeed, I get the eternal damnation treatment too.'

'You? Why?'

'That's a long story, and for another time.' He finished with the wipes and took a deep breath, then shook his head as if trying to wake himself up from a nap that had been too short to do its job. 'Right now we've got to get back on track, and that means finding Natalie. Have you got an overnight bag?'

'I've got a backpack. It's a bit shabby, but—'

'That'll be fine. Pack some clothes, a toothbrush and whatever else you need for the next few days.'

'Okay,' I said, and started heading for the bedroom, but then I paused when I decided that it might be a good idea to ask one more question. 'And where are we going, exactly?'

'London,' he said. 'We're going to London.'

CHAPTER SEVEN

At this point in my life, I could have counted the number of times that I'd been to London on one finger. That had been a school trip which had consisted largely of several long and extremely dull hours wandering around the British Art Museum, bookmarked by several equally long hours that were spent sending and receiving spitballs across the aisle of a National Express coach as we traveled to and from the capital. The best bit of that whole day had been catching a glimpse of my art teacher's bra as she bent over to grab an apple from her handbag, but apart from the tantalising cleavage of Miss Turner there was little about the trip that I remembered with any fondness. Now, over two decades later, I was going to London again, but this time it wasn't just to stare at pictures that I didn't appreciate, or at an ample bosom that I did. This time it was to save the world.

We had patched up the doorway to my flat as best we could by hammering the larger remnants of the door back into place, and then filling the gaps with various bits of the broken coffee table. I had told Perry that I thought we should at least call the landlord to let him know about the damage, but he had insisted that we didn't have the time to worry about such trivialities.

'If we don't find Natalie, and soon, there won't be anything for the landlord to worry about,' he had said. 'There won't be a landlord at all, come to that.'

Having learned the hard way that Perry did seem to know what he was talking about at least some of the time, I had dropped the subject, and less than an hour later we stepped onto the platform at Brighton train station.

The passengers who were already waiting for the next train to London seemed perfectly oblivious to the fact that I was on a mission, and to the gravity of it. An ageing station employee, who looked like he had just swallowed a moth, was alternately checking his watch and looking at a clipboard he was carrying. A group of a dozen or so commuters in business suits stood alongside each other with their briefcases hanging by their legs, but were careful to keep their eyes on their smartphones and evening newspapers, lest a misplaced glance should cause havoc by triggering a conversation. A trio of young teenage girls at the far end of the platform stood giggling over some article in the latest issue of Cosmopolitan magazine. It was all very normal. Mundane, in fact. The only thing that might possibly have struck anyone as being slightly unusual was the fact that the man in the white suit standing next to me was idly but expertly rolling a silver dollar back and forth across the knuckles of his right hand.

'Nice trick,' I said, breaking the silence that had accompanied us since leaving the flat.

'Huh?' He looked at me as if surprised to see me standing there, then realised that I was referring to the coin and immediately put it in his pocket. 'It's easier than it looks,' he said. 'Just something I picked up in Vegas.'

I was going to ask if he'd been there on business or pleasure, but that's when the tannoy crackled to life and announced the imminent arrival of our train. The passengers on the platform shuffled forward a pace or two in readiness, whilst I grabbed my backpack and slung it over my shoulder. The train arrived, we waited for passengers to disembark and then I followed Perry on board. He slid into a window seat in the first vacant table bay that he came to, and I settled down opposite him.

'So are there any other nasty surprises that I can look forward to?' I asked when the train lurched into motion.

'Say what?'

Considering that it was so late in the day, the table between us was surprisingly clean, so I leaned forward to avoid being overheard by any of the other passengers in the coach. Fortunately, the nearest one—a portly guy with pebble-shaped spectacles—was a couple of seats away and engrossed in a Stephen King paperback.

'This Doran Salt bloke suddenly turning up and trashing the place. You didn't seem all that surprised, but you didn't warn me, so are there any other things that you're keeping quiet about?'

He shook his head. 'The deal is pretty simple,' he said. 'If you succeed in your quest then we all live happily ever after and God herself might even crack a smile... though I doubt it.'

'And if I fail?'

'Then we're all screwed and Salt wins control of the universe for a thousand years.'

'Why Salt?'

'Because of who he is. Didn't you work out his name yet?'

'I've been a bit busy,' I said. 'The only thing I've been able to come up with so far is Rant Loads, but that doesn't sound much better than Doran Salt.'

Perry rolled his eyes as if he were listening to an imbecile, so I did my best to think a little harder.

'Lord Santa?' I suggested after two more minutes of intensive letter-juggling.

'That's probably a little too festive for him, but you're getting warmer,' Perry said. 'Now try raising the temperature even more, and don't stop until you get to the scorching flames of hell itself.'

His instructions puzzled me for a moment, but then the anagram finally clicked into place and I felt the blood drain from my face.

Perry nodded. 'Yeah, that's the one.'

I felt sick. The idea that Doran Salt was none other than Lord Satan, and that the devil himself had paid me a personal visit and threatened to destroy me, was both terrifying and difficult for me to get my head around.

'So if we fail he really takes over the whole universe? For a thousand years?'

Perry nodded solemnly.

'And then?'

'And then God starts over from scratch with another big bang.'

It sounded like an extreme solution, but then all of this was a bit extreme as far as my rational mind was concerned. Every bit of my experience since jumping from Brighton Pier had been ludicrous, nonsensical and pretty much impossible. Unfortunately, it had also been very real—a fact that my tormented brain was having lots of trouble processing.

'It might be a good idea for me to run through the rules with you,' Perry suggested. 'Just to clarify things.'

'Go ahead,' I said. 'I might as well know what I'm in for.'

He gave a nod of satisfaction, then reached into the inside pocket of his jacket to remove a small piece of paper, which he unfolded carefully.

'Okay, there are three main rules that you need to be aware of. First, you'll be pleased to know that Salt can't physically harm either you or Natalie. If he could then, believe me, you'd both be dead by now.'

'Well, that's a relief,' I said, forcing a weak smile.

'Yeah, but only for as long as he continues to play by the rules. And let's face it, he hasn't got a great track record in that department.'

In many respects, Perry Barr was a lot like the Lord of the Old Testament, because whatever he gaveth in one moment, he seemed to taketh away in the next.

'Second,' he continued, reading from the slip of paper, 'you can only succeed in your mission by getting Natalie to kiss you without invitation and by her own volition.' He looked up. 'And it has to be a real kiss.'

'Which means?'

'Which means that it can't just be a quick peck on the cheek. It has to be a real, meaningful thing.'

'You're talking tongues and stuff?'

'I'm talking about feelings, Gary, not saliva. This rule is

just saying that the kiss has to be heartfelt. It has to be motivated by love. She has to mean it with every fibre of her being.'

'Ah, okay,' I said. The odds of me succeeding seemed to be dwindling with every passing second. 'And what's rule number three?'

'You can't tell Natalie anything about the mission. In other words, you can't just go up to her and say that we're all doomed if she doesn't fall in love with you. Basically, the third rule exists to reinforce the second one. Capiche?'

I nodded. Understanding the rules wasn't a problem, but how the hell I would be able to pull this thing off without breaking them was another matter entirely. As if sensing my growing feelings of trepidation, he took the picture of Natalie from his pocket and placed it in front of me.

'Take that, and just focus on Natalie. Make her your prime motivation and you'll do yourself a lot of favours.'

'That shouldn't be too hard,' I said. 'She's perfect.'

'Yeah,' he grinned. It was the first time he'd smiled properly since Vinnie had roughed him up several hours earlier. 'She's clever, too. A bestselling author, no less.'

My brain processed the job description as a series of images: books, fingers tapping away at a keyboard, more books, a red carpet, the rapid flashing of cameras, even more books...

'You're kidding,' I said finally, the magnitude of her implied success now beginning to sink in.

'I kid you not. That's why she's in London. She has a book signing tomorrow.'

Success. Class. Style. Money. Flawless beauty. An insatiable appetite for kinky sex... Bestselling authors probably had all of those traits and more, and I imagined that Natalie had them in abundance.

'So why would she fall for me?' I asked, but I didn't actually realise that I had voiced the question out loud until Perry responded to it.

'Why wouldn't she?'

'You just told me exactly why she wouldn't. She's a bestselling author. That means she's probably used to a five-star lifestyle... and she looks like a goddess. What do I have to offer someone like her?'

Perry shrugged. 'There must be something or she wouldn't have been assigned as your soul mate.'

'Maybe *She* made a mistake,' I said, rolling my eyes heavenward.

'You really have no confidence in yourself at all, do you?'

The tone of his voice told me that it wasn't a jibe, but a straightforward observation, and as usual it was disheart-eningly accurate.

'My entire life amounts to nothing,' I admitted. 'Poor background, no higher education, crap excuse for a job... I can't just ignore all of that and suddenly have confidence, you know.'

'Sure you can,' he said. 'So what if your life was crap and you used to be a loser and a jerk?'

I didn't recall calling myself a jerk.

'You just have to move on and choose not to be a loser or a jerk in the future. If I could do it then so can you, believe me.'

He turned his head towards the window and began watching the landscape roll by. The slight but clearly discernible frown on his face suggested that he was now following his own train of thought, so I decided to try and pull him right back to the here and now.

'So, what's the plan?' I asked.

The question broke his momentary introspection and he turned back to me. 'We get to London, check into a hotel for the night, and then we get you some decent clothes first thing in the morning.'

'Clothes? For what?'

'For making a good impression,' he said. He waved vaguely at the worn denim jacket that I had thrown over an even older T-shirt just before setting off from the train station. 'I'm all for the homeless grunge thing that you have going on there, but we only get one shot at this, and some new threads won't hurt your chances any. Like they say, clothes make the man.'

It was a phrase that I'd read somewhere once, probably in one of the old copies of GQ that I was in the habit of flicking through whilst waiting for a doctor's appointment. I didn't know exactly what it meant, but it sounded like there could be at least some grain of truth to it. Whether new clothes would make anything new out of me personally was another thing altogether.

'And after the new clothes... then what?'

'Then we go to meet Natalie at the book signing.'

'And?'

'And, that's it.'

'That's the plan? I just show up and say hello?'

'Do you have any better ideas?'

It would have been really good to have responded with a whole raft of better ideas, but I couldn't come up with even one, so I simply shook my head.

'Look, she's your soul mate,' Perry said. 'She's bound to connect with you on some level.'

'Yeah,' I nodded. 'But I need her to connect with me on the lips, and I don't see that happening in a bookstore full of her fans the moment she lays eyes on me.'

'Neither do I, and that's why you need to invite her out for a coffee or something. Dinner, maybe.'

I nodded without conviction. 'That might work.'

'Trust me,' he said. 'You'll be fine.'

CHAPTER EIGHT

We arrived in London at just after nine that night and took a short cab ride from Victoria Station to a hotel which, according to the driver, was just a ten minute walk away from Buckingham Palace. My experience of hotels up to this point in my life wasn't vast, but I could tell at first glance that this one was something special. The place looked huge, for a start, and the people who were walking in and out of the large glass doors at the front of the building were the well-dressed, well-manicured and well-heeled types who wouldn't normally be seen in the same postcode as me, let alone the same building.

'Do we need to stay here, particularly?' I asked Perry after he'd paid the cab driver and watched him pull away towards his next fare.

Perry, still looking flamboyant in his 'not of this world' white suit, gazed up at the building and grinned. 'We're here on recommendation,' he said. 'Kinda majestic, I think.' He looked at me, concerned. 'Don't you like it?'

'It looks very impressive,' I said. 'But these places aren't cheap, and when it comes to cash-flow...' I felt too embarrassed to finish the sentence. Here I was, in my mid-thirties, and I was just as broke as I had been when I'd left school at sixteen. It wasn't that I hadn't wanted to succeed in life, you understand. It was just that—yes, you guessed it—I'd failed miserably.

Perry rested a paternal hand on my shoulder. 'Don't equate having money with having value,' he said. 'Do that and you might as well be one of them.' He nodded towards a group of slick young City boys who were emerging from the hotel, cackling among themselves like a pack of inebriated morons.

'Maybe, but we still need to pay to stay here. And then there's the whole buying new clothes thing that you've got planned for tomorrow...'

'You're on a mission,' he said. 'Nobody is expecting you to cover the expenses that are associated with it. The Lady Upstairs is taking care of all that.'

'Okay,' I conceded, suddenly feeling a bit more relaxed about the situation. 'In that case, this place looks as good as they get.'

Perry nodded, satisfied with my verdict, and walked up the steps to the entrance. A doorman doffed his hat and opened the door for us—something that I didn't think actually happened in real life—and a moment later we were standing in the main lobby. If the exterior of the building had given a hint of opulence, then the interior, with its antique leather seats, gilded ornamental ceiling and highly polished marble floor, positively reeked of it.

'You wait here, and I'll get us checked in,' Perry said,

and without waiting for a response he strolled over to the main desk.

I watched as he beamed a smile at the receptionist, pointed at her name badge and made some kind of comment about it. The distance between me and the desk on the other side of the lobby meant that I couldn't hear exactly what he had said, but whatever it was had got the receptionist giggling like a schoolgirl within all of ten seconds. Perry grinned at her reaction, shrugged and then said something else, causing the receptionist to laugh out loud and then blush when she realised that she'd let her mask of professionalism slip so quickly and so easily. Perry had charm, I'd give him that, and if he ever found a way of bottling his charisma and selling it on the free market, he'd be set for life.

'Okay, it's a done deal,' he said when he returned a couple of minutes later. He threw a key card in my direction, which I caught and slipped into my pocket. 'Some diva had a tantrum and trashed our suite the last time she visited, so it's all been refitted like new,' he grinned. 'Lucky us.'

The suite was situated on the top floor. The decor was modern, rather than traditional, but its black-and-chrome theme was very nicely executed, and there was more space here than in every room of my flat put together. A central lounge area was equipped with a leather sofa, two matching armchairs, a large glass coffee table and a big-screen TV that must have been six feet wide at the very least. An illuminated private bar occupied one whole end wall, and a grand piano sat silently at the opposite end of the room. A grand piano, for God's sake.

'The doors there lead to the bedrooms,' Perry said, indicating two doors at the piano end of the room. 'They're both doubles and *en suite*, so take your pick and I'll bunk down in the other.'

'Bunk down?' I snorted. 'You don't bunk down in a place like this. You die of overindulgence.'

'Maybe,' he chuckled. 'But what a way to go, eh?'

After taking a look at both bedrooms and discovering that they were both pretty much identical, I opted for the one on the left. I spent a few minutes taking some essentials out of my backpack and generally settling in, then returned to the main lounge area. Perry didn't have anything to unpack, and so he had started making the most of the room service, ordering himself a full three-course meal followed by a variety of cheeses. He encouraged me to do the same, but my appetite for rich food wasn't particularly strong, so I settled for the hotel's soup of the day and a sandwich, both of which turned out to be far fancier than their straightforward menu descriptions had suggested.

We made small talk over dinner, commenting on the evening news broadcast that we were watching on television, and wondering if there would be anything about Natalie's book-signing on the local bulletin. There wasn't. After dinner we made use of the bar—me pulling myself a pint of bitter and Perry opting for soda water with ice—and then we settled ourselves into the armchairs for the evening. It was almost like a lock-in without a landlord.

'So, how exactly did you end up doing this?' I asked. 'You said it was a long story.'

'Figure of speech,' he said.

'But there's always a story.'

'Yeah.'

'What's yours, then?'

Perry stared at me for a long moment, then took a sip of his soda and set the glass down on the coffee table. 'Greed,' he said. 'That's my story.'

I nodded and waited for him to elaborate.

He shrugged and settled back into his seat. 'I had a pretty good life to begin with. I married young. Her name was Rita. Beautiful gal. Pure as snow. We had a couple of kids, and I took on a job as a sales rep for the North Carolina Brush Company. That involved me traveling from state to state selling brooms, mops and all kinds of other cleaning supplies to homes and businesses across the country. The money was okay because I was an okay salesman, but it wasn't enough to fund the kind of lifestyle that I thought I deserved.'

'How do you mean?'

'I wanted my life to be special,' he said. 'I wanted the big house, flash car, Rolex watch, supersized bank balance... the works. I mean, there were other guys who had those things, so why not me? The problem was, I couldn't fund that kinda lifestyle by selling brushes.'

An image of a half-naked woman helping to advertise some miracle diet pill flashed up on the TV screen, distracting us both, so I leaned over to grab the remote on the table and pushed the off button.

'So what did you do?' I asked, not wanting Perry to close up now that I'd finally got him talking.

'I went to Vegas,' he said. 'There was a big sales convention being held there. The kind of event that they used to arrange to keep us enthusiastic about selling the products. The sessions started at nine in the morning and finished at five in the afternoon, and that gave us a whole lot of time to have some fun at the gambling tables. On my first night there, I got lucky at the craps table and turned a few dollars into fifty bucks. That might not sound like much today, but back then it was pretty good, and I figured that if I could do the same thing every night I'd go home a couple of hundred dollars better off.'

'But you didn't,' I guessed.

He shook his head. 'I lost it all the next night and started chasing. By the end of the week I was down three hundred bucks and had to pawn my watch for the train ride home. I should have stopped there, but I didn't. From then on, I played in every casino I could find in every town I visited for work. Craps, blackjack, poker—I played them all, and always with a glass of bourbon in my hand. Sometimes I won, and that helped me to believe I could keep on winning, but then I'd lose whatever profit I'd made, and more besides. Within three years, I was drinking a bottle of bourbon a day and I was forty grand in the hole. That was ten times my annual income, including commissions.'

'Jesus.'

'Yeah,' he said. 'Anyway, to cut to the chase, it all came to a head in 1953—on the twenty-seventh of March, to be even more specific. It just happened to be a Friday, a week-long conference had just finished and I decided to celebrate by spending some time at the card tables. I ended up betting beyond my means, as usual, and I lost my wedding ring.'

'Ah.'

'It wasn't worth much in cash terms, and I'd pretty much pawned and lost everything else of value before then, but when the ring went the same way... I dunno. It had sentimental value, y'know? And losing it suddenly made me realise how low I'd sunk. I'd lied to Rita about all the other losses, and she'd trusted me enough to not even question my explanations, but there was no way that I could look her in the eye and lie about the ring as well.'

He paused to take a sip of his soda water. He was staring into space, as if looking back into his own past, and there was an expression of intense sadness on his face. The silence was almost tangible, and I tried to think of some words of consolation with which I could break it, but how could I console him about something like that?

'I had a life insurance policy that was worth a few grand,' he continued, 'so I figured I should try and do the right thing by my family. I was never going to win big. I couldn't even win small. The more I played, the more I lost. And they deserved more. Much more. The policy meant that I was worth more dead than alive, so I said to hell with it, and called time on the whole thing. I went back to my hotel, got drunk, opened the window, stepped out onto the balcony, and jumped. Eleven floors later, I was history. I haven't touched a drop of alcohol since.'

I watched as he drained his glass, and I realised right then, perhaps for the first time in my life, that I wasn't the only person in the world who had been less than satisfied with his situation. Actually, my situation had been pretty good if I compared it with the one that Perry had just described. My life had been dull, for sure, but it had never been as dark as how I imagined his must have been during those final months.

'I'm sorry, Perry,' I said. 'And I'm sorry that I can't think of anything better to say than that.'

'Hey, what's done is done.' He forced a smile, but it didn't convince either of us. 'Bottom line is that we have a lot more in common than you might think. I threw away my life and so did you. The only difference is in what we have to do to make up for it. Your mission is to save the world, and right now mine is to give you all the help that I can. We're in this together, and if we fail, we're screwed—not just you and me, but everybody else on this planet.'

I nodded, but my head was swimming with questions. I wanted to ask Perry if he knew how Rita and the rest of his family had coped after his suicide, and whether either of his two kids were still alive. I also wanted to know how many other missions he'd been assigned to over the last sixty years or so. But all of that would have to wait. Right now wasn't the time to make him feel any worse than he already did.

'Are you finished with that?' He was gazing at the remote control for the television.

'Course,' I said. 'Help yourself.'

A moment later he was channel-hopping. I knew that he was just trying to distract himself from the painful memories that had been dragged up, but I could hardly blame him. I'd have done exactly the same in his position.

'How about that,' he said with a smile. 'The game has just started, live and direct.'

He rose from his seat, grabbed his empty glass from

the table and walked over to the bar to refill it with soda water.

'I don't really understand American football,' I said when he returned to his armchair a few moments later. 'Rugby, yes, but American football...'

'Better settle in then, kid,' he said. 'You've got a lot to learn.'

CHAPTER NINE

Until now, I had never really given much consideration to the way I looked. Don't get me wrong, I wasn't a complete slob. I shaved and showered every morning like most other civilised people, and I even ran a comb through my hair every now and again, if time permitted, but excessive preening and worrying about the subtler nuances of fashion just wasn't my thing. On those occasions when I had ever picked up a copy of a men's style magazine, such as GQ or Esquire, it had been in the hope that I'd get a glimpse of some particularly fit actress in a state of undress, and not at all for the metrosexual articles about hair care products, or which set of cufflinks would be the best match for this season's sealskin brogues. My wardrobe, if you want to call it that, consisted of several pairs of bog-standard jeans, a dozen or so T-shirts, and a couple of pairs of trainers. As far as I was concerned, that was all a thirty-something single guy needed if he didn't have an office job, but Perry disagreed quite passionately.

'Image is everything,' he said as we walked down Oxford Street.

It was just after ten in the morning. The sky was blue and the streets of central London were already bustling with Sunday-morning commuters, wide-eyed tourists and tired old touts selling cheap souvenirs at exaggerated prices from battered suitcases. We were heading towards some place that Perry had mentioned over breakfast in the hotel a couple of hours earlier. He hadn't specified exactly what that place was, but he'd told me that it was one we needed to visit as a matter of urgency.

'If you look too casual, it makes people think that you're a slacker,' he continued. 'Those old jeans of yours say that you don't have any self-discipline, and your scruffy T-shirts say that you couldn't care less.' He glanced over to look me up and down, then looked away again, shaking his head in disgust. 'The way you dress, you might as well have the word anarchist tattooed across your forehead.'

I looked down at myself. I was wearing a pair of slightly faded blue jeans and an old grey T-shirt, but nothing that I considered particularly scruffy.

'You might be overstating things a bit,' I said.

'You think?'

'Wearing jeans and a T-shirt doesn't make me an anarchist. Maybe that's how people thought about things back in the fifties, but times have changed. We have smart-casual, dress-down Fridays...'

'Do you think those jeans are smart?'

'Not particularly, no.'

'Is today a Friday?'

'No.'

'Well, then,' he said, as if my responses had proven his point quite nicely. 'But we'll get to your clothes later. Right now you need a haircut.' He stopped walking and nodded to the door of a barber shop called Trim for Him. 'In here.'

'What's wrong with my hair?' I asked, looking at my reflection in the glass of the door. 'I only had it cut a few weeks ago.'

'Did you do it yourself?'

'No, Jesus...'

'Well, you couldn't have done much worse if you had,' he said, and he nodded to the door once again.

A couple of days earlier I would have responded to that kind of sleight with a few choice words plucked directly from my extensive knowledge of Anglo-Saxon, but things were different now. I had a mission to carry out, and since that mission involved getting a total stranger to plant a passionate one on me, it made sense to make the target—namely, *moi*—as visually appealing as I possibly could.

I sighed and entered the barber shop.

Should anyone ever decide to make a movie of my life, the next few hours of that morning in London could probably be condensed into a three-minute montage sequence. Rocky Balboa had his famous training montage, the A-Team guys had their weekly 'let's make a bazooka from a vacuum cleaner and six empty dog food cans' montage, and I would have a 'Gary gets a makeover' montage orchestrated by Perry Barr.

It started in Trim for Him, where Perry ordered the barber to give me a 'classic gents' wash, cut and dry. I couldn't believe how much hair the guy chopped off when he got down to it, or how long it took him to complete the three-stage process (almost an hour), but when I finally saw the finished look in the mirror I couldn't help but be impressed by his work. I wasn't quite so impressed with what he charged for the job, but I wasn't paying, so I didn't see the point of making a fuss about it.

Next came half an hour in a gentleman's fragrance store. I didn't know that such stores existed, and I quickly got bored with Perry droning on about the various differences between woody, leather and *Fougère* base notes, but the clerk seemed impressed, and they were both keen for me to sniff fragrance strips and spray numerous samples on my hands and wrists until we came across something that all three of us liked. My hands stank like a perfumer's boudoir by the time we'd finished (although I am only speculating on that matter), but we eventually bought two bottles of the carefully selected *eau de toilette* and a generous handful of matching toiletries. I didn't see exactly how much that lot cost, but I'm pretty sure that the same amount of cash would have bought me a new games console if we'd shopped elsewhere.

Then came the wardrobe overhaul. This was an even more time-consuming process which took place in a variety of 'gentlemen only' stores, all of which were far too expensive for their own good. At first, I tried expressing my opinions about the items of clothing that were presented to me, but every time I said that something looked good, Perry screwed up his face and shook his head sympathetically. It was almost as if my liking something was evidence that it was shit, and so I soon learned to keep my mouth shut and let him do his thing. The number of shirts, suits, ties and shoes that I tried on must have been in the dozens, and we seemed to be buying around half of them. That seemed a bit excessive, given that the universe was at risk of ending long before I'd have the chance to wear it all, but Perry clearly liked buying the stuff, and Ms Fire and Brimstone was still footing the bill, so no harm was done.

Perry had arranged for most of the shops to send our earlier purchases directly to our hotel so that we wouldn't have to carry them around with us, but when we were in what turned out to be the last store of the morning—which was almost four hours after I'd first stepped into the Trim for Him place—he told the clerk to send my old clothes and shoes to the hotel instead.

'What's the point of that?' I asked. I was still doing up the cufflinks on the latest blue shirt that he'd insisted I try, and by now I was getting used to the task, though why anyone still bothered with cufflinks was beyond me.

'Because we're going to see Natalie.'

'When?'

He looked at his watch. 'In twenty minutes. So you need to wear this suit to go.' He held up the suit jacket and I weaved myself into it as if I'd been doing this kind of thing for years.

'We're not going back to the hotel first?'

He shook his head. 'No time.'

It was then that the reality of the situation swept over me like a bloody big tidal wave. I just wasn't prepared for things to be proceeding at this pace. Talking about meeting my divinely appointed soul mate face-to-face was one thing, but actually doing it was quite another, and my stomach started rolling over like an indecisive porn star.

Seemingly oblivious to my inner turmoil, Perry grabbed my shoulders and turned me around to face the full-length dress mirror. 'There you go,' he said. 'Whaddaya think?'

I looked at the reflection staring back at me, and to be honest, the first thing I thought was: *Who the hell is that?* Considering the raw material that he'd had to begin with, Perry had worked wonders, and the guy in the mirror was now a fairly good-looking bloke who would have been right at home on the pages of any style magazine you could care to name. It was me, but it was an upgraded me. It was me as James Bond. Navy suit, light blue shirt, navy tie and shoes that were so well-polished I'd be able to check my flies without breaking my stride.

'Amazing what a few new threads can do, isn't it?' Perry admired his handiwork in the mirror and grinned, satisfied. 'I swear, you could be the ugliest pup on the planet and you'd still be able to score in that outfit.'

'Cheers,' I said, not quite sure whether or not I should feel offended.

'Anytime,' he nodded. 'Let's just hope that Natalie feels the same way.'

CHAPTER TEN

Queues are an intrinsic part of British life, and I had seen plenty of them in supermarkets, as well as at bus stops, night clubs and cinemas, but I had never encountered a queue of people waiting to get into a bookshop. Not in real life, anyway. Yet that was exactly what we found when we approached Waterstones on Piccadilly, where I estimated that there were at least a hundred prospective book-buyers all waiting patiently for their turn to walk through its doors.

A large sign in the bookshop window read: NATALIE KAYLAN—TODAY AT 2PM. There was no other text, just the name and the time, as if any explanation about who Natalie Kaylan was, or what she wrote about, would be completely redundant. Of course, it then occurred to me that the woman I was here to meet didn't need any introduction as far as the other people queuing were concerned. It was probably only me, having read far too little and far too narrowly over the last couple of decades, who hadn't heard of this particular bestselling author, at least until my very recent successful-but-still-failed suicide bid.

'She's popular,' I said as we tagged onto the end of the queue.

'Your powers of deduction are impressive.' Perry tapped the shoulder of the woman standing in front of him, who was engrossed in a paperback, and when she turned around he pointed at me with his chin. 'The Force is strong in this one,' he said.

The woman looked me up and down as if I were a strange curiosity, then nodded politely at Perry and quickly returned to her reading.

Perry smiled to himself.

'So, what does she write?' I asked.

'Bodice rippers,' he said. 'Heaving bosoms, quivering loins, fluttering love lips, that kinda thing.'

'And I'm supposed to buy a copy and ask her to sign it for me?'

'Well, it doesn't have to be for you, does it?'

'True,' I said. 'Maybe I'll tell her it's for my mum.'

'You're an orphan.'

'I'm well aware of that,' I said. 'I'm just trying to be creative, that's all.'

'Creativity is fine. But try to avoid telling any outright lies that might come back and bite you in the ass.'

The queue was shuffling forward at a slow but steady pace. I estimated that we would probably be waiting for at least twenty minutes before we would be able to set foot inside the bookshop, and the delay wasn't helping my nerves one bit. A couple of women who had been eavesdropping on our conversation in a less than discreet manner turned away when I glanced at them. Suddenly aware that my words were being monitored by the people around us, I leaned closer to Perry and lowered my voice. 'I still wish we had a better plan than just asking her out.'

'We did have a better plan,' he said. 'We had the perfect plan. She was going to knock on your door like a damsel in distress and you were going to help her out. It was your decision to drop everything and kill yourself which messed that one up, so this is Plan B. Deal with it.'

I was tempted to ask how he could be so sure that I would have helped Natalie if she'd knocked on my door as God, in her infinite wisdom, had intended, but there was no point. Of course I would have helped her. I might not be a lot of things, but I'm a decent sort of bloke, when push comes to shove, and if her car had needed pushing and shoving then I would have offered my assistance will-ingly. If being helpful in that way would have also led to something more intimate then, well... who was I to complain about the architecture of the cosmos?

Fifteen minutes later, which was a tad earlier than I had estimated, the queue had moved forward nicely and we finally entered the bookshop itself. It was a pretty impressive place, with six floors and more books than anyone could possibly read in a single lifetime, but it was difficult to see much else thanks to the queue of people that was snaking gradually through a maze of elegant rope barriers.

The mass of people in the store meant that I had no idea where Natalie was situated, but I could hear one particular woman laughing gently from time to time, and my gut tightened at the thought that the laugh just might belong to her. To the person who I was going to ask out within moments of saying hello for the very first time.

Oh, God.

It wasn't that I didn't want to ask her out. Of course I did. After seeing her photo, I'd have been mad to not want to. Or gay. But just because you want to ask someone out doesn't mean that you should go ahead and do it. No, no, no. You first have to think things through, and weigh things up, rationally.

To start with, you have to give the potential recipient of the invitation a numerical rating out of ten. If Natalie looked anything like she did in her picture, and with a personality to match, she would definitely be a ten. Then, you have to give yourself an honest rating. I'd probably consider myself to be a five or a six, under normal circumstances, but after Perry's makeover I was deserving of a pretty solid seven. Finally, you compare the two ratings, and if hers is higher than yours by anything more than one point, you forget the whole thing and go for a beer instead. If you ignore that approach then you're just punching out of your league, and the inevitable rejection will make you regret your unfounded optimism pretty damn quickly.

On that basis, I should have been running to the nearest pub, rather than setting myself up for disappointment.

'You'll be fine,' Perry said. 'You look great.'

The way he seemed to read my mind was unnerving, but it had to be said that his pep talk of six words did help a bit. I straightened myself up, pulled my shoulders back and took a deep breath. That's when the crowd of people in front of me finally dissolved, and I saw her face-to-face for the very first time.

Holy hell.

She looked like an angel.

Yes, I'm quite aware that I'm speaking in clichés, but honest to God, the moment I saw her looking back at me, everything changed. For a moment—probably one of the longest moments in my life—I became completely unaware of my surroundings. All I could hear was the sound of my own breathing. All I could see was her smile. It was the most gorgeous smile I'd ever seen, with the most kissable lips imaginable. And her eyes... Jesus. They weren't eyes at all. They were perfect pools of baby blue that made me want to jump into them and splash around for the rest of my days.

Perry nudged me back to reality with a discreet elbow to my ribs. Natalie was sitting at a wide table with her pen poised over the title page of her latest book, and there were a dozen or so more hardback copies stacked to her left. It was then that I realised I was standing with my mouth hanging open, so I quickly closed it and forced it into a smile that would, I hoped, appear cool and impressive. Natalie giggled at the effort, but not in a way that made me feel at all self-conscious. If anything, it put me right at ease.

She stared at me for a moment longer, as if thinking about something, but then shook her head in defeat. 'I'm sorry, you just look very familiar to me for some reason. Do I know you from somewhere?'

Her voice was warm and sweet, like honey. God, she was gorgeous.

'Not yet,' I said. 'But the day is young.' I have no idea where that particular phrase came from. Damn me and my lack of chat-up lines.

Another smile—have I mentioned that she was absolutely gorgeous?—and then she turned her attention back to the open book. 'Is it for you?'

'No, it's for my mother,' I lied. 'She's a big fan. The biggest. She's read everything you've ever written.'

'Really?' she asked, raising an eyebrow. 'Even the first one?'

'The first one is her favourite.'

'That's surprising,' she said. 'Most of my older readers didn't really appreciate the hardcore bondage scenes in the first one.'

'Bondage?'

'Yes,' she nodded. 'The scene where the seven little men had their way with the heroine in the Grand Duke's orgy room got me a damning review in the Times Literary Supplement, I can tell you.'

It was then that I realised just how uncomfortably warm it was. I ran a finger under my shirt collar to try and get some air to my neck. Did she mean little men as in generally short blokes, or did she mean men with restricted growth? Or were the men only little in the trouser department? In which case, why were they in an orgy room? And who the hell was the Grand Duke? Not the one from York, surely?

'I'm teasing you, silly,' she giggled. 'The first book was the tamest of the lot.'

'Ah, right,' I said, and I tried to laugh at the joke, but I would have found it a lot funnier if she'd picked on someone else apart from me and the little people.

'So what's her name?'

'Whose name?'

'Your mother's.'

'My mother is dea—'

'Desdemona,' Perry interrupted as he elbowed me in the ribs once again, but this time more forcefully. 'Desdemona Fenton.'

Natalie looked at him, and then back at me, presumably to see if I was going to object to his sudden interference.

'He's with me,' I said.

'Lucky him,' she smiled, and she started autographing the book.

Perry shot me an encouraging glance.

This was it. Now or never. Do or die.

'Look, I know that this is probably a bit sudden,' I said, 'but would you like to go out sometime?'

She closed the book and handed it to me. 'Out?'

'For dinner.'

'Ah... I'm sorry, but I already have dinner plans.' She nodded sideways to a woman with shoulder-length ash-blonde hair, who I hadn't even noticed was standing a couple of feet to her right. 'With my agent.'

'Maybe a coffee then?'

She shook her head apologetically.

'Well, do you have a card or anything? So I can contact you?'

'I'm sorry, I don't,' she said. 'But I do chat with fans on my website from time to time. The address is on the back of the book.'

'Right,' I said, and that was when the readers behind me must have decided that I'd been hogging their favourite author for long enough, because they lurched forward as one and—before I knew what was happening —completely squeezed me out of the picture. I kept my eyes on Natalie the whole time as I was pushed back through the crowd, but eventually the mass of bodies obscured my line of sight, and my encounter with the gorgeous Ms Kaylan ended just as suddenly as it had begun.

'Well, we're screwed now,' I said when we eventually stepped out of the bookstore with the newly purchased bodice-ripper. It was still sunny outside, but rather than lifting my spirits, the brightness of the day only served to make my own predicament feel all the more gloomy by comparison.

'At least you've made first contact,' Perry said.

I glared at him. 'She's not a bloody alien, you know.'

'I didn't say she was. I'm just saying that you aren't strangers any more.'

'Okay,' I nodded. 'But, strangers or not, we're still screwed.'

'We'll come up with something,' he said. 'We have to.'

When you're watching a movie, it can be pretty inspiring to hear someone expressing a sense of never-say-die optimism in spite of ridiculously overwhelming odds. Unfortunately, when someone does it in real life, and they aren't the one who actually has to overcome those odds, it can really get on your tits. I opened my mouth to make Perry aware of this, but was quickly interrupted by the ash-blonde woman who had been standing guard over Natalie just a couple of minutes earlier. She was an attractive woman with a bright, friendly face who appeared to be in her late forties or thereabouts.

'Awfully sorry to butt in,' she said, 'but Natalie asked me to catch up with you and give you this.'

She handed me a slip of notepaper and I unfolded it

warily as Perry not-so-discreetly peered at the contents. It said: *I'm staying at The Grysek. Dinner at 8pm?*

'Isn't she having dinner with you?' I asked the woman.

She shook her head. 'Natalie says that to everyone who asks her out during a signing. I've never known her say yes to anyone, until now.'

'And your name would be?' Perry asked with what I assume was his most debonair smile.

'Jenny,' the woman said. 'Jenny Marsh.' She looked back at me. 'So can I tell Natalie that you'll be there?'

'God, yes,' I said, and then I caught myself just in the nick of time, and tried to continue in a more refined tone. 'Please tell her that I wouldn't miss it for the world.'

'Great, well, that's great then,' Jenny grinned. 'I'll go and tell her that. Thanks.'

We watched her go back inside the bookshop, and then Perry turned to slap me on the back with what I felt was a little too much enthusiasm. 'Nice going, kid. You almost blew it at the final fence, but it looks like you've gotten yourself a date after all.'

'Yeah,' I said. And then it hit me. In the space of five minutes I'd met the most gorgeous woman on the face of the earth, I'd asked her out and she'd actually accepted. It was clearly time for my nerves to kick in again. 'Oh shit, what do I do now?'

'Come on, you've been on dates before,' he laughed.

I didn't laugh with him.

His jovial features melted. 'You've never been on a date?'

'Of course I've been on a date.'

He looked relieved to hear that.

'It's just been a while, that's all.'

'How long, exactly?'

I pretended to think hard about his question, but it didn't require any thought at all. 'A couple of years,' I said. 'Maybe five or so.'

For a moment he regarded me with a look of sympathy—the kind of look that you might give an otherwise cute-looking rabbit after discovering that it has myxomatosis—and then he checked his watch. 'Okay,' he said. 'We've got a few hours. Hopefully that should be enough.'

'Enough for what?'

'To bring you up to speed.'

'You're an expert in dating all of a sudden?'

'No, but I know a man who is. Come on.' He started walking briskly up the street, in the general direction of our hotel.

'Where are we going?' I asked, but he didn't answer. He didn't even acknowledge hearing the question. So I did what any sick rabbit might do in the same situation, and I followed him regardless.

CHAPTER ELEVEN

When an Agent of the Council of the Most High God tells you with the utmost air of confidence that he knows a man who is an expert on a given topic, it is perfectly reasonable, in my opinion, to have rather high expectations. As I once again allowed Perry to lead the way through the streets of London, I considered the various possibilities.

Maybe we were on our way to meet another agent who specialised in the art of romance. Or perhaps it was someone even more important, such as an Archangel of Booty, who I imagined might be a bit like the legendary Hugh Hefner with wings. No, that would be sex, not romance. Cupid? Was Cupid a real angel or just a mythical figure, like Santa Claus? Now that my previously held notions of myth and reality had already been challenged thanks to a certain meeting with God—a being I had hitherto assumed to be little more than a figment of childish imagination—the idea that Cupid might also be at work somewhere was almost viable. And since I was making a mental list of possibilities, was Saint Valentine a real saint or did the greeting card industry simply adopt him in order to emotionally blackmail people into spending far too much cash on ridiculously mushy nonsense?

As you can gather, I was leaving no stone unturned as I pondered who Perry might be referring to when he said that he knew an expert in dating, but none of that speculative rumination prepared me for the moment when the white-suited agent led me into a store and announced our arrival.

'Okay, this is it,' he said.

I looked around. There were shelves. Lots of shelves. All of them were stocked with thin plastic cases according to their category: Action, Comedy, Horror, Drama and more. Brightly coloured signs hung from the ceiling, silently screaming the name of the store—presumably for the benefit of those who have a tendency to blindly wander into whichever building happens to be nearest when it rains.

'DVDs?' I asked. 'You brought me to look at DVDs? Do you really think we have time to watch movies?'

He ignored my questions and wandered off to the Classics section of the store, his eyes slowly scanning the shelves from left to right, top to bottom. An obese woman was standing nearby with her skinny boyfriend, pointing out all of the titles that she'd seen. 'Seen it, seen it, seen it, seen it, seen it, that was brilliant—I wouldn't mind seeing it again sometime, but not tonight—seen it, seen it...' and on she continued. Obviously, spending your whole waking life sitting on your arse watching movies is the thing to do if you're committed to getting the whole obesity thing down pat.

'There,' Perry said as he pulled a particularly thick DVD case from one of the lower shelves. 'Someone had put it in the wrong place.'

I snatched the case from his hands. It was a triple bill of movies, and two of the titles were in black and white.

'Never heard of them,' I said, giving the case straight back to him.

'Well, you're watching them anyway.'

'Your solution to my lack of dating prowess is to buy movies?'

'No, my solution is for you to learn from a master.' He pointed to the guy on the cover of the DVD, who was sporting a dinner suit and impeccable hair. 'Mr Cary Grant, no less.'

'But those films are ancient.' I flipped the case over in his hand and pointed at the dates on the back. 'See? These are from the forties and fifties.'

'It's not the dates of the films that matter, but the man himself,' Perry said. 'If we can get some of Cary Grant's magic to rub off on you before tonight, your chances with Natalie will be terrific.'

I wasn't convinced. 'That might have been the case sixty or seventy years ago, but it's a different world these days.'

'Trust me,' he said. 'Old-fashioned romance never gets old.'

And with that, he left his pithy Hallmark greeting hanging in the air and went to pay for the movie.

According to the details on the back of the DVD case, the

movie which Perry selected for us to watch when we were back at the hotel suite had a running time of less than two hours, but it felt much longer. It wasn't that the film was bad—on the contrary, I was surprised to find that I quite enjoyed it—but Perry was pausing it every five minutes to highlight various points which seemed quite trivial.

'Look at the way he stands with his left hand in his pocket,' he said at one point, imitating the pose as he did so. Then, about five minutes later, it was, 'Listen to the way he stresses that *ah* sound whenever he says darling. *Dahhling.*'

On each occasion, I simply nodded to feign understanding, at which point he would return the nod, satisfied, and allow the movie to resume.

When the end credits finally rolled, Perry rose from his seat, clicked off the TV and stood expectantly in the middle of the room.

'Well?'

'Well, what?'

'What did you learn?'

'That special effects are way better than they used to be?'

The frown on his face told me that I had given him the wrong answer.

'You were supposed to be learning how to be a gentleman,' he said. 'Why d'you think I kept pausing the movie and pointing things out?'

'I know he was a gentleman,' I said. 'But I honestly don't think that I could pull that off.'

'Sure you can. All you have to do is use the same formula that Cary Grant used.'

'There's a formula?'

He let out an exasperated sigh, like a football that had just been punctured. 'It's the same formula that guarantees success in any area of life,' he said. 'Look the part, talk the talk and walk the walk.'

Surprisingly, that almost sounded interesting.

'Say that again,' I said. 'Slowly, this time.'

'First you have to look the part, and that means you have to dress like a gentleman. We took care of all that this morning. The suit we bought you?' He made a circle with his thumb and forefinger and punched the OK sign into the air for emphasis. 'It's perfect.'

I had to nod my agreement there. Although wearing the suit took some getting used to (let's face it, nothing is quite as comfortable as an old pair of jeans and a T-shirt) I couldn't deny that it did make me look good.

'Next, you need to talk the talk.'

'Which means?'

'Avoid slang and speak properly. And definitely no profanities.'

'Fuck no. Profanities are slangy bastards, aren't they?'

He flared his nostrils at me but didn't take the bait. 'You'll note that Cary Grant said *dahhling* a lot.'

'You did point that out six or seven times,' I said.

'Well, you should do that too. Chicks love that stuff.'

I considered telling him that using the word 'chicks' when referring to today's women was probably some kind of crime against equality, but the last thing I wanted to do was prolong the conversation, so I let it slide.

'Last, but not least, you need to walk the walk.'

'You mean follow through on what I say, right? Live up to my own hype? Because actions speak louder than words and all that?'

'No,' he said, and his facial expression suggested that I was mad for even putting the idea forward. 'I mean you need to walk the walk. The Cary Grant walk. You need to swagger.'

'Swagger?'

He nodded. 'That's right. Like this.'

Perry demonstrated what he considered to be the Cary Grant swagger by pacing to the end of the room and back again, his left hand nonchalantly half-tucked into the pocket of his blazer and his chin tilted up into the air. He almost looked like he was sniffing something sublime, and I had to tighten my lips to avoid cracking up at the sight.

He swaggered back to the centre of the room. 'Come on,' he said. 'It's your turn.'

'Really?' I groaned. 'Do I have to?'

'No, you don't have to. The creator of the entire frickin' universe is sitting upstairs with a lightning bolt aimed at your ass, but I'm sure she'll understand if you have better things to do.'

People are too sarcastic for their own good, sometimes, but he had a point. There was a kind of purpose to all of this, and a big part of that purpose for me was to avoid personal annihilation, so taking his advice might not be such a bad idea, even if it did mean embarrassing myself.

Still reluctant, but now willing to be a bit more compliant, I got up from my seat and swaggered to the far end of the room and back again, just as Perry had demonstrated. It was actually a lot easier than I had expected.

'What the hell was that?' he asked, wiping the proud smile off my face with just five words.

'You said to swagger.'

'Yeah, but not like that. Like this.' He demonstrated the swagger once again. 'Remember?'

'That's exactly how I did it!'

'No, you walked like a platypus with a limp,' he said. 'You have to stand up tall and straight. Be confident. Show me that you're proud of yourself.'

And there was the problem.

'I'm Gary Fenton, remember?'

'Well, pretend that you're somebody else,' he said. 'Somebody good.'

Okay, I'll admit that I flinched at that comment—who wouldn't?—but Perry didn't appear to realise that he had just slighted me, and I wasn't going to point it out to him.

'Imagine that you're the tallest guy in the room,' he continued. 'Imagine that you're strong, confident, charming, intelligent, eloquent and damn good looking. You're Cary Grant. You're the most impressive guy in all of London. You're a success at everything you do. Hell, you probably even shit gold when you take a dump.'

'Nice imagery,' I said.

'Just try it.'

Taking a deep breath, I closed my eyes and imagined myself being ten feet tall, but I didn't go so far as to visualise myself excreting golden nuggets. Even so, when I opened my eyes and had another go at swaggering back and forth there was a definite improvement. I could feel it in myself and I could also see it in the smile that Perry was beaming.

'Attaboy,' he said. 'You've got it.'

'And that's it? You think that if I just say *dahhling* and swagger properly, the girl of my dreams is suddenly going to be hot to trot?'

'It worked for Cary Grant, didn't it?'

'But that was a movie!'

He put a paternal hand on my shoulder and looked me square in the eyes. 'You wanna know a secret, kid? Your entire goddamned life is just one big movie, so if you don't take charge and start directing it for yourself, some other schmuck will direct it for you.'

CHAPTER TWELVE

It wasn't until our arrival at Natalie's hotel, where we were greeted by a doorman wearing a top hat and white gloves, that I realised just how out of place I was going to be. Yes, I looked the part, thanks to Perry's familiarity with ridiculously expensive menswear boutiques, and the doorman nodded respectfully, as if I was exactly the type of person who ought to be visiting the establishment that he so conscientiously guarded, but on the inside my intestines were playing a bizarre game of Twister. I don't know if it was the opulence of the environment, as it had been when we had first arrived at our own hotel the day before, or just the prospect of spending time with Natalie on a one-to-one basis, but I suddenly felt like some kind of imposter. Like a fish out of water.

Perry was seemingly oblivious to my nervousness. He walked into the lobby of The Grysek at exactly the same moment that I did, but as usual, he barely seemed to notice the extravagant surroundings. He simply checked his watch and nodded happily.

'Okay. We're here, and we're bang on time. Can't have a better start than that.'

'I feel out of place,' I said, speaking the words quietly so that only Perry would hear them.

'That's just your mind playing tricks on you,' he said. 'You deserve to be here just as much as anyone else. Confidence, remember?'

'Yeah,' I said, and I found myself standing a little straighter as I did so. 'Confidence.'

Perry nudged me and discreetly shoved a credit card into my hand. 'No expense is to be spared.' He pointed up to the heavens with his eyes. 'And those are Her orders, not mine.'

I nodded and slid the card into the pocket of my suit jacket. 'Thanks. What's the PIN number?'

'The year you were born.'

'Handy.'

'We didn't want you to forget and experience any kind of embarrassment,' he said. 'But if anything does go wrong, I'll be in the bar, so just give me a shout.'

'I will,' I said. 'And thanks again. For all your help, I mean. I guess it's down to me now.'

'You'll be fine,' he told me. 'And she's about to walk right in, so I'll make myself scarce. Good luck, kid.'

I glanced over to the door and saw that Natalie and Jenny were already being greeted by the doorman. I quickly turned back to Perry to comment on how gorgeous she looked, but he had already done a vanishing act. Whether the speed of his departure had been made possible by his angelic status or a sudden thirst for soda water, I had no idea.

What I did know, without a shadow of a doubt, was

that Natalie really did look incredible. She was wearing a figure-hugging black dress (whether it should be described as a cocktail dress, an evening dress, or some other kind of dress, I'm not really qualified to say) and she had her hair tied up in a bun, revealing a soft, slender neck adorned with a thin silver choker. When she saw me, which was just a moment or two after entering the lobby, she smiled, and I caught myself grinning back at her like a besotted schoolboy. It was as if every problem in my life had suddenly evaporated into nothingness, and all that was left was perfect in every way. I did my best to remain calm as she approached me.

'Hello,' she said. 'I haven't kept you waiting long, I hope.'

'No, I've only been here a minute or two myself.' I took her hand and bent down to kiss it politely, hoping desperately that Perry had been right about old-fashioned manners never going out of style. She was still smiling when I straightened up, so I took that as a good sign. 'You look stunning.'

'Don't mind me,' Jenny chimed. 'I'm only here for contractual purposes, so I'll be in the bar if anyone needs me.'

We exchanged friendly nods and she walked off towards the bar. I wondered for a second how she would get on with Perry when she found him hiding out there too, but that particular train of thought was derailed before it had even left the station, thanks to a deeply tanned chap who approached Natalie with a beaming smile and a ridiculously thin pencil moustache.

'You are looking exquisite, as always, *Mademoiselle.*'

He had an accent so thick that I couldn't help but

doubt its authenticity. Not that I should have been thinking about other people being fake. Not in my situation. Pot, kettle, and all that.

'And you're as charming as ever,' she replied as she mock-curtsied. 'This is Pierre,' she told me. 'He's the best *maitre d'* in the whole of London, bar none.'

He acknowledged me with a bow of the head, and I returned the gesture.

'Come,' he said. 'For these words, you and your handsome guest will dine at the finest table of all, and it will be a privilege for me to attend to both of you personally.'

He led us through the restaurant to a secluded table for two, and was just about to pull out a chair for Natalie when I stepped forward to do the honours myself.

'Please, allow me,' I said in my best Cary Grant accent.

Pierre immediately gave way with a respectful bow of the head, and Natalie sat down.

'That's very nice of you,' she said. 'I like old-fashioned manners.'

'Quite right, too,' I replied, and I took my seat opposite her.

Pierre smoothly produced a menu for each of us and then bowed yet again. 'If you will excuse me for a few moments, I will leave you to make your selections.' He turned with a smart flourish and promptly marched back towards the lobby.

I tried my best to look smooth and sophisticated as I opened the heavy leather-bound menu and scanned the delights on offer.

'Jesus.'

And then I realised that I'd spoken out loud.

Shit! Shit! Shit! Shit! Shit!

'Is something wrong?' Natalie asked, her eyes wide with surprise at my one-word outburst.

Yes, there was something wrong. Quite apart from the fact that I'd just uttered a very ungentlemanly—and probably blasphemous—expletive, the prices in this place were beyond ridiculous. I'd only scanned the starter menu and some of the options cost more than I used to earn in a whole morning at Piece o' Hut. God knew what the main courses would run to. I had the Bank of Heaven credit card or whatever it was in my pocket, of course, but still... it was the principle of the thing.

That was when I caught myself.

Cary Grant. Cary Grant. Cary Grant.

'I'm sorry?' I asked, with what I hoped would come across as an air of absent-mindedness. 'Oh, nothing at all... *dahhling*... I was just thinking aloud, that's all. About the cheeses. They have some quite exquisite cheeses here.'

Natalie nodded enthusiastically. 'They really do, don't they?'

What. A. Save.

Although much of the menu appeared to be written in French, which was a language I had never really had much call for, ordering the meal was a lot easier than I expected, thanks in large part to Natalie giving me her personal recommendations and Pierre helpfully suggesting the most appropriate wine to compliment each course. When he had jotted our choices into his notepad, he bowed his head—that must have been the fourth time since I'd first laid eyes on his thin black moustache—and left with another promise to return shortly.

'There isn't much point in me asking if you come here

often,' I said. 'You're one of the fixtures, by the look of things.'

She laughed at the observation. 'It feels that way some-times. I come here five or six times a year, I suppose. Whenever I have appearances booked in the area. It's like a home from home by now.'

'And where is home? If you don't mind me asking?'

'Lewes, in East Sussex,' she said.

'You're kidding?'

Come on Fenton, I chided myself. Cary Grant doesn't talk like that.

'No, why?' she asked. 'Don't you approve?'

'I know it quite well, that's all. I live in Brighton.'

Her eyes widened a little. 'Really? That's so weird.'

'It is?'

'Yes,' she nodded. 'I was there the day before yesterday, teaching a session at a creative writing conference. I could have used a friend there because my car broke down on the night I came back. You could have given me a push!'

I laughed at her joke, but I wasn't laughing on the inside. Although she wasn't aware of it, Natalie had just confirmed everything that I'd been told since jumping from the pier on Friday night. Everything really had been arranged for us to meet, exactly as Perry had said, right down to her car breaking down. Although I'd been working on the assumption that his story was more accu-rate than not, having an outsider confirm his words suddenly made everything seem far more... I don't know. Serious, I suppose.

'So, what brings you to London this week?' she asked. 'Are you here on business too?'

'Well...' I stumbled, wondering how to answer, or how

Cary Grant might answer if he were the one sitting in my seat.

'That was a silly question really,' she said, oblivious to my predicament. 'I don't even know what you do for a living.'

I knew that it would be wrong to tell an outright lie just to try and impress her, but I decided that it wouldn't be such a big sin to phrase the truth about my 'career' in such a way that it sounded at least a little more impressive than it really was.

'I don't know myself, right now,' I said. 'I used to work in the retail sector, but I recently decided to move on from that side of things. I'm currently just enjoying the break as I plan my next step.'

'So you're taking a sabbatical,' she said. 'Good for you. I think more people should have the guts to do something like that.'

'You do?'

'Absolutely. Most people don't think about anything much. Not properly. They just drift through life from day to day, earning money to pay the bills so that they can earn more money and pay more bills. It's a bit of a tread-mill as far as I can see.'

'For most people, yes, but you write fiction for a living. That must give you more satisfaction than a regular career, surely?'

'The writing itself does, yes,' she conceded. 'But all of the other stuff that goes along with it—the meetings, the conferences, the book signings—it can all get quite tiring. I mean I love my fans, obviously, but I feel happiest when I'm at home, sitting at my desk.'

I smiled at the thought of her sitting at a broad oak

desk in a book-lined room with shafts of sunlight streaming in from a nearby window. 'You sound like a born writer to me.'

'Maybe,' she said, 'although I didn't realise that writing was what I really wanted to do until I was already halfway through a psychology degree at Cambridge. I finished the degree, and I suppose it's a subject that comes in handy now and again, but I'd have studied something a bit more relevant if I'd known earlier.'

I was both impressed and daunted by this revelation. Not only was she a bestselling author, but she also had a degree in psychology, and she'd got it from Cambridge University, of all places. I'd had a strong inkling that I was punching above my weight long before this conversation, but I was now pretty much certain of it. If I hadn't been on a quest to save the world I might have excused myself and made a run for the bar right there and then, but I had a job to do, and retreating like a coward wasn't an option, so I chose instead to steel myself with a generous sip of wine.

'When did you get your first book published?' I asked when I put the glass down.

'Six years ago,' she said.

'And how many have you written so far?'

'The latest one is my sixth.'

'A book a year,' I said, demonstrating my mastery of basic arithmetic. 'That's impressive. What keeps you going?'

'I just have a need to tell stories, I suppose.'

'And they're always romantic ones? Boy meets girl type of thing?'

She nodded. 'Maybe if I had some real romance in my

life then I wouldn't find it necessary to keep writing about it.'

'Come on, that can't be true.'

Natalie furrowed her brow. 'What can't?'

'That you don't have any real romance in your life,' I said. 'I mean, look at you. You're gorgeous, funny, intelligent... There isn't a man in this room who wouldn't give his right arm to spend some time with you.'

She smiled and her cheeks flushed a little. It was a look that made my insides turn to warm honey.

'You're very sweet,' she said.

'I'm just being honest, that's all.'

We both reached for our wine glasses at the same time, and I decided that I'd do something particularly Cary Grant before the waiter brought our food. 'A toast,' I said, and I raised my glass. 'To honesty.'

She looked at me with an open mouth for a long moment, and I was beginning to think that my deliberate gesture was one too many, but then her lips curled into a smile. 'And romance,' she added.

We didn't take our eyes off each other as we drank our toast, and in that moment, I realised that Cary Grant had been a total bloody genius.

CHAPTER THIRTEEN

After a perfectly enjoyable starter and main course, I excused myself and made my way to the men's room, where I sent a text message to Perry to let him know that now would be a good moment for the half-time team talk. He entered the room a minute or two later and immediately went to wash his hands at the row of basins, motioning for me to stand next to him and do likewise.

'We'll keep this quick because you don't want to keep Natalie waiting for a second longer than necessary,' he said, looking at my reflection in the large mirror that ran across the length of the wall in front of us.

'Okay.'

'So, how's it going?'

'Good, I think.'

'You think?'

'Well, I don't really have much experience with this kind of thing, but she seems to be having a nice time, and I think she likes me.'

'What makes you say that?'

'I'm not sure,' I said, and I turned the question over in my mind, searching for whatever evidence I could think of to support what might easily have been a purely optimistic response. 'Because she's smiling a lot?'

'Great. That's great, kid,' he said with a grin. 'And how's the conversation? Are there any long pauses, or is it flowing, nice and smooth?'

'It was a bit awkward for me at the beginning, what with the nerves and everything.'

'And now?' he asked, his face suddenly sporting a look of concern.

'Now we're getting on like a house on fire. You know, laughing and joking about everything and nothing. It's more like we're old friends than complete strangers.'

His trademark grin reappeared, causing the expression of concern to vanish as quickly as an Essex girl's resolve after three white rum cocktails.

'Perfect!' he said. He shook the water from his hands, walked over to one of the three dryers on the side wall and started rubbing his palms together under the hot air. 'All you have to do now is keep it going and trust chemistry to take care of the rest.'

'You make it sound so easy.' I grabbed a handful of paper towels from a nearby dispenser and quickly dried my own hands. I wondered for a moment whether God would be annoyed about us damaging the environment with our unnecessary ablutions, then decided that she probably had more important things on her mind, given that there might soon be no environment for her to worry about in the first place.

'Well, it's working so far, isn't it?'

'Yeah, I suppose,' I said. 'But when am I supposed to make my move, exactly? For the kiss, I mean...'

'Don't even think about that. Not yet. If you rush things you could seriously mess up the whole shebang. We only have one shot at this, so just focus on being charming and friendly, and take things one step at a time. Capiche?'

'Sure. Perfectly capiche,' I said, but in truth, his reminder that I only had one shot jangled my nerves a bit. I looked at my reflection, forced a smile at the suited Gary Fenton looking back at me—at Fenton 2.0, if you like— and steadied myself with another slow, deep breath.

'Good.' He opened the door and motioned for me to exit the men's room first, which I did.

'And how are you getting on with her agent?' I asked, almost as an aside.

'Jenny, you mean? Oh, we're getting on fine. Fine. Just fine.'

A broad grin appeared on his face. It was the kind of grin that would, in other circumstances, cause even the most liberal of parents to lock up their daughters.

'Oh my, I've wanted to taste that for such a long time.'

Whilst Natalie's comment might have sounded perfectly plausible in a hardcore porn movie, she was actually referring to the exotic-looking chocolate mousse that she had ordered for dessert. Multiple layers of differently shaded chocolate, praline and creams had been served in a tall glass with a long spoon, and her first taste of the dish had clearly met with her approval.

'Here, try some,' she said, reloading her spoon and offering it to me.

'Thanks, but I'll take your word for it,' I said, because I may not be the most mature of men, but I'm definitely past the spoon-feeding stage.

'Oh, come on. Live a little. You know you want to.'

Her words were innocent, but the way she looked at me when she spoke gave them an entirely different meaning. Or, at least, that's what my genital region thought, and my genital region—like that of any other red-blooded male—had the ability to pull rank on virtually every other part of my person. That's why I leaned forward, opened my mouth and took the food from her spoon.

Natalie smiled broadly and relaxed back in her seat. 'Good, isn't it?'

'Very,' I said, and I wasn't lying. Then it dawned on me that Cary Grant would probably offer to return the dessert-sharing favour. 'Want to try some New York cheesecake?'

She nodded and leaned forward, opening her mouth for me to feed her a modest forkful. Her gaze didn't leave mine until she closed her eyes in an expression of mock ecstasy.

'Hmmm,' she said finally. 'That's really good too.'

The whole 'you taste mine and I'll taste yours' thing only lasted a few seconds, but it somehow gave the rest of the dinner—and the conversation we shared—a far more intimate tone. Although we didn't quite interrogate each other over the next forty-five minutes or so, we did touch on quite a few personal topics, including our hugely disappointing experiences with past relationships, our shared dislike of politicians of all persuasions and our mutual appreciation for the humble Pot Noodle.

'That surprises me,' I said.

'What, that I prefer the Chicken and Mushroom to the Bombay Bad Boy?'

'No, that you actually know what a Pot Noodle is.'

'Why wouldn't I?'

'Because you're a bestselling author who went to Cambridge?'

'Ah, that,' she said, reaching for her glass. She took a sip of wine, then set it back on the table and shrugged. 'Well, I only went to Cambridge because I worked my lady-nuts off to win a scholarship. And if you take away the fancy clothes that my agent insists I wear to signings then I'm—'

'Naked?' I quipped.

'Just a simple working girl,' she said, smiling coyly.

'Ah, right.' I grinned, pleased with her response.

'And what about you?' she asked.

'What about me?'

'Who are you when you take off the Armani suit?'

Being reminded that I was actually wearing an Armani suit made me feel a little self-conscious. Earlier, it had made sense for me to present myself in the best possible light, but now, having learned a lot more about Natalie, I really didn't want to make a false impression. I mean, sure, the hair and the clothes made me look good on the outside, but they didn't reflect who I was on the inside. Externally, it appeared that I was someone who dressed and carried himself with charm and elegance, like Cary Grant. But internally... well, I was still the same Gary

Fenton who had found so little meaning in his life that he'd decided to end it all by jumping from Brighton Pier.

I wanted to confess right there and then, and tell her that I wasn't the kind of guy who would normally be seen dead in a suit, even an Armani, and that I'd need to stack shelves at Piece o' Hut for quite some time before I could even afford to buy one under my own steam. Had the fate of the entire universe not been resting on my ability to make a positive impression, I would have told her all of that, but my appearance had been carefully manicured for a reason, and I couldn't risk blowing it with such blatantly honest admissions.

'I'm just a working-class guy with big ideas,' I said, finally, and I silently congratulated myself on having managed to answer her question honestly without undoing all of the hard work that Perry had put into the creation of my stylish facade.

'Big ideas, eh? Are you telling me that Gary Fenton wants to save the world?'

I felt my face flush.

'Well, somebody has to,' I replied in a cool, calm tone that concealed my inner discomfort. 'So, why not me?'

She looked at me for a long moment, her head cocked to one side as if she was trying to figure me out, and then she chuckled softly. 'You're a funny guy, you know that?'

I shrugged and reached for my drink.

'Handsome, too,' she said.

Fortunately, I'd swallowed the mouthful of wine just a moment before she added those words, so instead of spluttering the burgundy liquid all over the crisp white tablecloth, I simply coughed in surprise.

'Steady,' I said when I'd composed myself. 'That's just the drink talking.'

'No, I don't think so,' she said. 'I thought you were handsome when you came into the bookstore for the signing, and I hadn't touched a drop all day.'

I looked at her carefully, half-expecting her to crack up or shout 'Sucker!' at some point, but it didn't happen. It was true that she was smiling, but it wasn't because she was joking, and when I realised that she really was saying that she fancied me, I felt an overwhelming urge to say something back.

'You are fucking gorgeous.'

She looked at me with her mouth open for a long moment, and then burst out laughing. I wondered why, at first, but then it hit me.

I'd dropped the f-bomb.

After putting in all of that effort—getting the haircut, buying the clothes, watching the Cary Grant movie, listening to Perry's line-by-line pointers, practicing the walk, pulling out her chair, bluffing my way through the menu and trying to come across like an all-round gentleman—I'd let the mask slip, and the real Gary Fenton had, rather characteristically, thrown a fuck-shaped spanner in the works.

So, now what?

Apologise, you fool.

'I'm terribly sorry,' I said in the most polite accent I could muster. 'That was unforgivably rude of me.'

'Why?' she asked. 'Didn't you mean it?'

'Well... of course I meant it. I just didn't intend for it to come out like that.'

'I'm quite glad that it did.'

I looked at her, surprised by the comment, but she continued without skipping a beat.

'Everywhere I go, people are always so nice and deferential. Publishers, promoters, bookshop managers, readers... they're all so careful to present themselves in the best possible light. To hear someone just say what they think without censoring themselves is a pretty rare thing for me.'

'So you aren't offended?'

'That you think I'm fucking gorgeous? Not at all. In fact, I think I'm pretty fucking flattered.'

She smiled broadly at me, her eyes twinkling mischievously, and I couldn't help but to grin right back at her. Rather than completely ruining my chances, it looked like my slip of the tongue might have actually worked in my favour. All I had to do now was hope that things would keep going in the same direction.

We finished our meal about half an hour later, after a coffee liqueur and a conversation that had become increasingly flirtatious as it had progressed. By the time we reunited with Perry and Jenny in the lobby, I was grinning from ear to ear, and every time Natalie glanced at me, she smiled in a way that made my insides feel like they were lighting up.

Perry took me to one side as Natalie and Jenny started chatting between themselves.

He raised his eyebrows expectantly. 'Well?'

'Incredible,' I said.

'That good?'

'Unbelievably good. The whole evening went way better than I had any right to expect.'

'Attaboy,' he said, slapping me hard on the back of the shoulder. 'So, when are you seeing her next?'

'I don't know,' I said. 'We didn't discuss that.'

His face dropped, like I'd just told him that I'd accidentally killed his pet rabbit.

'Say that again.'

'We didn't discuss it.'

'Why the hell not?' he asked, his voice now twice as loud and his face twice as red as it had been a moment earlier.

'Because I didn't know I was supposed to, did I?' I replied, allowing my own voice to increase a few decibels. The guy may have been a divinely appointed Agent of the Council, but that didn't give him the right to be a jerk about it.

He looked back over his shoulder to make sure that the girls hadn't heard our exchange, and then quickly ushered me behind a tall green floor plant, presumably for privacy and not so that we could check it for aphids.

'Of course you were supposed to. What do you think the whole point of the dinner was?'

'To get to know each other,' I said.

'Yes, but also to get to the next base. Which means arranging to see each other again as soon as humanly possible, and not letting her walk off into the sunset leaving the future of all mankind in the balance.'

'Ah, yes,' I said, suddenly remembering the bigger picture. 'We were getting along so well that I forgot about that side of things.'

'Forgot?' His eyes widened, and he opened his mouth

again as if to unleash a torrent of abuse on me, but then Natalie appeared from the other side of the foliage and he quickly closed his lips tight to force a polite smile.

'Sorry to interrupt you gentlemen, but we're heading up to my suite for nightcaps and we wondered if you'd both like to join us?'

I looked at Perry in a deliberately smug manner.

'Thank you, we'd love to,' I said, not waiting for him to respond. 'Lead the way, and we'll be right behind you.'

She nodded, pleased, and started walking with Jenny towards the bank of elevators on the other side of the lobby.

'See, it all worked out fine in the end,' I said.

Perry wrinkled his nose, as though my words were polluting the air. 'You caught a lucky break, kid,' he said. 'And that happens, once in a while. But if you count on luck to save your ass every time you need it, you're gonna end up sorely disappointed, believe me. I've been there, remember?'

There was a thick and unmistakable note of disapproval in his voice, but it also had the warmth of a paternal warning. Back in his gambling days, Perry had relied on luck to the point where it had destroyed him, and so it was only to be expected that he wouldn't want me to start doing the same.

'Yeah,' I said. 'I'm sorry.'

He accepted the apology with a nod. 'Come on,' he said. 'We have some nightcaps to enjoy.'

We rode the elevator to the top floor of the hotel, waited for the ding that announced our arrival, and then stepped out into the thickly carpeted corridor. Natalie and Jenny continued to lead the way, leaving Perry and me to follow. The corridor was pleasantly silent after the piped lounge music of the elevator, but even that had been rather easy on the ears, and not at all like the painfully bad synth-pop covers that I was used to enduring at work.

I stole a sideways glance at Perry, who seemed to have relaxed a bit after our short but heated conversation in the lobby. I knew that I had let him down a bit by failing to think ahead and secure a follow-up to the dinner with Natalie, and I also knew that it really was sheer good luck that had saved my skin. Whilst I couldn't go back and undo my temporary lapse in concentration—and fortunately, I didn't need to—I could certainly try to do better in the future. We would go and have one or two drinks in Natalie's suite, and I would go back to playing the perfect gentleman, oozing the same kind of charm and grace that had, according to Perry, made Cary Grant one of the most popular leading men of the twentieth century.

We rounded a corner and slowed to a stop outside the only door in this part of the building, and then waited as Natalie dipped her hand into her purse to retrieve a key card. She held the card against the sensor to the right of the doorway, paused for the lock to click open and turned the door handle. Natalie entered the room first, Jenny followed close behind and Perry motioned for me to go in next. I wish he hadn't, because it meant that I was first on the scene when the lights went on and the two women screamed in unison.

'Less of the screaming, please. This isn't a bloody funfair.'

The voice belonged to Doran Salt, who was sitting on a large cream-coloured leather sofa on the opposite side of the room. He was pointing a handgun at a wide-eyed Natalie, who had instinctively raised her hands in the universal gesture of surrender. Vinnie, the gorilla-sized skinhead who had managed to trash my already trashy flat a couple of days earlier, sat beside Salt, his face bearing an inane grin.

Salt waved the gun at Jenny.

'You,' he said. 'Close the door.'

She looked at Perry, who was standing by the door and glowering at the devil. Reluctantly, the agent stepped aside and nodded for her to do as Salt had requested. The poor girl looked terrified. In fact, both girls did.

'If you're going to point that thing at anyone, point it at me,' I said. 'The girls have nothing to do with this.'

'Really?' Salt raised his eyebrows at me in a rather

condescending manner. 'I was under the impression that the delightful Ms Kaylan had everything to do with this.'

'I'm sorry?' Natalie said, clearly shocked that the guy with the gun knew her name. She turned to me, her brow furrowed. 'Is he with you?'

'No, not exactly,' I said.

'I'll do the talking, if you don't mind,' Salt snapped. He turned at a slight angle to look at Vinnie. 'It's come to something when even a pistol full of bullets fails to command respect, hasn't it?'

The skinhead nodded solemnly.

Salt sniffed. 'It's a sorry state of affairs,' he said. 'Makes you wonder what the world's coming to.'

Vinnie shrugged.

Salt sighed and turned back in our direction, then rose to his feet. 'Alright, this is what's going to happen,' he said. He was waving the gun around as he spoke. 'You're all going to do exactly as I say without a single word of protest. There is to be absolutely no resistance, no more screaming and no attempt at heroics. If any one of you breaks those rules then I will have no choice but to discharge the contents of this weapon into your fleshy parts without any further warning. Have I made myself clear?'

Natalie and Jenny nodded without hesitation. I glanced at Perry and we both exchanged the same look of helpless 'What choice do we have?' resignation before reluctantly nodding our own acknowledgment.

'Excellent,' Salt said. He waved the gun at Perry and me. 'You two, stand over there.' He indicated the centre of the room. 'Back-to-back. Hands by your sides.'

'I don't think so,' Perry protested. They were the only

words he had uttered since entering the room, and his voice was defiant.

Salt grabbed Natalie by the arm, span her around to face Perry and pushed the muzzle of his gun to her temple. He glared at the agent.

'Woah! Okay, okay!' Perry conceded.

He quickly walked to the centre of the room, and I followed suit. We stood back-to-back, as if we were about to walk twenty paces in opposite directions and fight an old-fashioned duel, but since neither of us had been given any weapons it was unlikely that such a showdown was on the agenda.

'Secure them,' Salt said.

'Yes, Boss,' Vinnie responded. He reached over the side of the sofa to grab something, then stood up and came towards us with several lengths of rope and a large reel of duct tape.

'Look, can't we discuss things first?' Perry asked. 'Like adults?'

Salt shook his head. 'There's nothing to discuss.'

'Great,' Perry huffed.

I turned my head away from Salt and the girls in an effort to communicate with Perry quietly. 'We don't just have to stand here and take this,' I muttered. 'He isn't allowed to hurt me or her, remember?'

'That's if he plays by the rules,' he countered. 'Do you really want to risk finding out if he will?'

He was right. Salt had a gun to Natalie's head and it would have been stupid to try anything clever. I turned back and looked at her, hoping that she would under-stand why we were just standing there and letting Vinnie bind our wrists behind our backs with duct tape.

When he had finished that part of the job, he bound the two of us together with lengths of rope around our ankles and waists. Natalie still had a look of panic in her eyes.

'Try to stay calm,' I said, doing my best to keep any tone of nervousness out of my voice. 'I won't let anything happen to you, I promise.'

Salt laughed. It was a deep, hearty laugh that made me realise just how ridiculous my assurance to Natalie must have sounded. Here I was, bound helplessly in the middle of the room, and I was making promises to keep her safe, even though I wouldn't have been able to scratch my own arse had my life depended on it.

'Laugh all you like,' Perry said. 'You haven't won yet.'

'No,' Salt agreed. 'But then, neither have you, and right now I think that the odds are leaning just a tad in my favour. Wouldn't you agree?'

Perry said nothing.

Natalie looked at me.

'Don't worry,' I silently mouthed to her, but she shook her head, unable to understand. 'Don't worry,' I mouthed a second time, but the communication was missed once again.

That was when Salt noticed me miming and rolled his eyes.

'Tape their mouths shut as well, Vinnie. It seems that Mr Fenton here is suffering from a sudden outbreak of charades.'

'Don't worry,' I said again, this time uttering the words out loud just before Vinnie slapped a wide strip of duct tape across my mouth. He did the same to Perry, then turned his attention back to his previous task, checking the strength of his rope knots to make sure that they were tight enough.

They were. We couldn't budge an inch.

'All done, Boss,' Vinnie said.

Salt grinned his approval. Natalie noticed his sharp canine teeth for the first time, and visibly paled.

'Perfect,' he said. He nodded in Jenny's direction. 'You take her and I'll take this one.'

He tightened his grip on Natalie as Vinnie lumbered over to Jenny and grabbed her by the arm, giving her a lecherous smile as he did so.

'Not a sound, remember?' Salt reminded the girls. He waved the pistol around again to remind them of the fact that it was still very much in his hand.

They nodded quickly.

Satisfied with their response, he escorted Natalie to the door and bundled her out into the hotel corridor. Vinnie followed with Jenny.

'Well, that was easy,' Salt said.

And that was when the door closed behind him, leaving me and Perry bound and duct-taped together in the middle of a now-empty room.

We stood motionless for a few moments, listening carefully. Salt continued talking to Vinnie in hushed tones as they made their way down the corridor, and then we heard the distant ding of the elevator arriving for them. That was our cue to begin struggling.

Vinnie might have looked like a steroid-fuelled Neanderthal, but his ability to secure us in such a way that we wouldn't be able to escape was, unfortunately, quite impressive. Our ankles and wrists had been given absolutely no room for manoeuvre, and the fact that we had also been secured to each other like conjoined twins meant that we couldn't coordinate our efforts. All we could do was strain against each other, pulling and grunting in a completely random and desperate manner until we were too exhausted to continue, which turned out to be just a couple of minutes later.

'Mm mmmm mm mmm mm mmm mmmm,' Perry muffled.

'Mmmm?' I asked. The duct tape didn't even allow us to open our lips, let alone say anything comprehensible, but we had an urgent need to communicate, and being secured back-to-back meant that some kind of audible exchange was our only option.

'M mmmm, mm mmmm mm mmm mm mmm mmmm.'

I tried to express my lack of understanding with a shrug, but I couldn't do so, for obvious reasons. Fortunately, the effort itself seemed to be enough to get my point across.

'Mmm,' Perry muffled, and he attempted to jump on the spot, which wasn't a particularly comfortable experience for me.

'Mm,' I groaned.

I heard him sigh heavily—it was quite possibly a sigh of exasperation—and then he resumed his effort to take charge of the situation through the medium of nondescript sounds. 'Mmm, mmm, mmmmm...' he muffled, as if counting *one, two, three...*, and then he tried to jump on the spot again. He followed that by leaning a little in the direction of the door.

'*Mm, mmmmm!*' I responded, suddenly getting his drift. He wanted us to jump in sync towards the door, presumably so that we could make our escape. Quite how he thought we would be able to grab the door handle and use it once we were there, I had no idea, but I figured we would cross that bridge—or not—when we got to it.

'*Mmmmm?*' he muffled.

'*Mm-mm,*' I replied, acknowledging that, yes, I was ready.

He took a deep breath, and then started counting down again. '*Mmm, mmm, mmmmm...*'

On the count of *mmmmm*, we both made an effort to jump in the direction of the door, and to my surprise, we actually succeeded. Granted, we only landed an inch or two away from our starting point, but it was progress.

When we had gathered ourselves together, Perry muffled another countdown, and we made another successful jump towards the door. Then we got brave and picked up the pace, with Perry counting down rapidly so that we could make more jumps in a shorter period of time.

Unfortunately, it was that overconfident haste which led to our undoing, because after half a dozen more jumps, and having covered only half the distance to the door, we lost our coordination and ended up crashing to the floor in a bound heap. Being unable to brace ourselves meant that the landing, which involved me falling onto my left side and Perry onto his right, was far harder than I had anticipated, and the thick pile of the carpet did little to cushion the impact.

Winded and weary, we remained motionless on the floor for a minute or so, before making an effort to get back to our feet. The problem with uprighting yourself from a position where you're lying on your side, with your arms and legs bound and another guy strapped to your back, is that it's virtually impossible, and after a few minutes of trying in vain we simply gave up.

'*Mmmm,*' Perry muffled.

I don't know exactly which word he was trying to utter, but I understood the gist of his communication, and I was pretty sure that I felt equally despondent. The big question now was how long it would take for us to figure a way out of our predicament.

I would like to say that the urgency of the situation motivated us to come up with an absolutely genius plan which enabled us to free ourselves in a noble, swift and incredibly dramatic fashion, but it didn't. We came up with a plan alright, and that was to use momentum to try and roll ourselves towards the hotel room door. We also succeeded in executing that plan, picking up several facial rug burns on the way. But then, once we had reached our objective, we reluctantly accepted that we literally had nowhere else to go.

Fortunately, the solution to our problem came and knocked on the door all by itself.

'This is the police. If you can hear me then please open up immediately.'

We couldn't open the door, for obvious reasons, but we could do the next best thing, which was to grunt as loud as our duct tape gags would allow. The action had the desired effect, and a moment later the door was open and a rather surprised policeman was looking down at us.

The policeman introduced himself as Constable Morris. He was a tall, lanky, ginger-haired chap in his late forties, and he didn't waste any time in removing the duct-tape strips from our mouths.

'Thank God,' Perry said. 'We need to report a kidnapping.'

Perry explained what had happened as Constable Morris started using the blade of his trusty Swiss Army Knife to cut through the ropes that were binding us. The questions came thick and fast from Morris, and we answered every one of them as truthfully as we could without actually mentioning the fact that the perpetrators of the crime were not quite normal human beings. Perry even suggested a car registration number that might prove useful to the investigation—a personalised plate that Salt had apparently used on previous occasions.

When we were completely free, Morris instructed us to take a seat on the sofa, and then he tapped the radio that was clipped to the breast pocket of his jacket and reported the incident to the station. We sat in silence for a few more minutes whilst he wrote up the details of the case in his small black notebook, and it was during that period of quiet that I realised I had a question of my own.

'Who called you?' I asked when he had flipped the notebook shut.

'The guests in the room below,' he said. 'They reported what they thought was some kind of domestic dispute. Lots of banging around, and so on. Hotel security were a bit put out that they hadn't been informed first, because they usually deal with any minor disturbances on the premises, but it looks like it was a police matter after all.'

A crackle of static punched the air and Morris responded instinctively, his hand quickly sweeping up to his radio so that he could respond with his call sign.

'Could you confirm the car registration you reported earlier, over?' a female voice asked.

'Affirmative. It was Hotel, Three, Lima, Lima, Eight, Three, November, Tango, over.'

'Thought so,' the voice responded. 'It's not in the DVLA database, but we have had one sighting of that vehicle. It was heading towards the Soho area, about twenty minutes ago.'

'Of course!' Perry said, his eyes wide. He stood up, then grabbed my arm and dragged me to my feet. 'Come on, we gotta go.'

'Where to?' I asked. 'What's in Soho? Do you know where they're going?'

Perry shot a cautious glance at Morris, who looked just as keen to hear the answer as I was, and then he turned to me and nodded.

'Yeah,' he said. 'They're going to Hell.'

Perry dragged me out of the hotel room and started running towards the elevator at the end of the corridor. I ran to keep up, and Constable Morris made a half-hearted attempt to do likewise, but he clearly wasn't as motivated as we were, because he was falling further behind with every stride.

'Slow down,' I told Perry. 'He can't keep up.'

'He's done all he can by finding out where their car was heading,' he replied. 'Now it's up to us.'

We reached the elevator and the doors opened just as soon as Perry had pressed his thumb to the call button. He stepped inside and quickly pulled me in after him, then jabbed the ground floor button a split second later.

'Hey now,' Morris said, panting for breath, but the elevator doors closed before he could finish his sentence.

Perry tapped his foot impatiently as the lift made its descent. His eyes were fixed on the floor indicator panel the whole time, and when the doors finally opened to the lobby, he was off running again. He looked like some kind of divinely appointed Forest Gump as he sidestepped bewildered hotel guests, made his way towards the exit and then charged out of the building.

By the time I caught up with him, he was already opening the door of a black taxi cab, and a few moments later we were on our way to an address in Soho that he had pretty much barked at the driver. I thought that Perry's abrupt manner was a bit uncalled for, to be honest, but the cabbie didn't seem to be too surprised by the American's attitude, and merely rolled his eyes at him through the rear view mirror. Perry was unaware of this because he was staring out of the passenger window. In the distance, I could see the iconic shape of Big Ben, its illuminated structure glowing proudly against a clear night sky.

'Where exactly are we going again?' I asked, settling back into the cushioned leather of the seat.

'Hell,' he said, still staring out of the window.

'In a black cab?'

He turned to face me. 'It's a club. Actually, it's a strip club. It used to be a popular hangout for fallen angels in the eighties.'

'And you reckon it's still there?'

He shrugged. 'We'll see.'

'I've never heard of any strip club called Hell.'

'Because it wasn't intended for mortals. It was more of a recreational hideout for the demonic fraternity.'

I nodded. A couple of days earlier, the suggestion that demons might be fraternising in a strip club in London would have sounded ridiculous, but the things that I'd encountered since trying to inhale the English Channel had helped to open my mind quite considerably. Not only did I now find myself believing that a strip club for demons might actually exist, but I also believed it enough to be concerned about the potential dangers of visiting such a place.

'Let's say that this Hell club is still there,' I said, trying to think of a way to continue the sentence without sounding like a complete chicken. 'Do you actually think it's a good idea for us to be going there on our own?'

'Not really. But what's the alternative? Leave Natalie and Jenny to take care of themselves? Play the fiddle and watch Rome burn?' His questions were clearly rhetorical, so he didn't wait for me to answer them. Instead, he shuffled forward to address the cab driver. 'How much longer, pal?'

'About ten more minutes, squire,' the cabbie replied.

Perry nodded and sat back in his seat, his gaze returning to the night-time scenery that was rolling by outside.

I looked at the clock on the dashboard. The glowing green digits told me that it was just after one in the morning. Five hours earlier, I'd been trying my hardest to make Natalie think that I was the perfect gentleman, but now she was probably thinking something else entirely. I'd been given one shot, and as usual, I'd messed up royally.

'It was going so well.' I was talking to myself more than anyone else. 'She really seemed to like me.'

'Of course she liked you. She's your soul mate.'

'I should have gone straight for the kiss at the end of the meal...'

Perry shifted around to face me again. 'Look, there was no way you could have known that Salt was lying in wait. And, as I told you before, you can't rush these things.

If you'd gone for the kiss right there and then, you might have blown your chances completely. You did the right thing.'

'Maybe.'

'For sure. Just try and stay positive.'

'That's easier said than done.'

'I won't argue with you on that score,' he said, 'but we've both been given a chance to redeem ourselves here, so we'd be assholes to not give it everything we've got.'

I nodded, thinking back once again to the story he'd told me about the gambling problems which had led him to leap from his eleventh-floor hotel balcony—an event that had taken place decades before I had even been conceived.

'How many missions have you been on since...' I shrugged, hoping that the remainder of my unfinished sentence would speak for itself.

'This is my fiftieth,' he said.

'Your fiftieth?' The surprise in my voice was impossible to disguise. 'That's like...' I tried to figure out the average number of missions that he must have completed each year since committing suicide in 1953, but it was already late and so I soon abandoned the project, choosing to pose a different question instead. 'Why so many?'

'Because that's how many She decided was needed to pay for my crime,' he said. 'Lucky me, huh? So I worked my ass off, and I notched up my forty-ninth mission last year. I was almost at the finish line, and so close to having another shot at living a decent life that I could almost taste it.' He fell silent for a few moments, frowning at the thought. 'And then you decided to end it all. Which means that none of the other missions really count for anything, because if we don't succeed in this one then pretty soon there won't be any world left for me to go back to.'

His tone was one of sadness rather than blame, but the sense of guilt that I was beginning to feel was unmistakable. When I'd jumped from the pier, my only concern had been for myself and my desire to escape my own boredom with life. I really hadn't thought about any of the consequences of my suicide.

I hadn't believed in any kind of afterlife back then, of course, but there were still plenty of woo-woo-free consequences that I should have considered. How the group of youths on the pier might have felt after seeing a guy jump to his death, for example. Or how my selfish act could have affected any poor sod who would eventually find my drowned corpse on the beach the next day. The fact that the actual consequences had been even more far-reaching, and that my suicide had set in motion a chain of events that could end things for absolutely everyone—including Perry, who had worked so hard to secure his own second chance at life—was beginning to weigh very heavy on my conscience.

'I'm sorry,' I said. 'For doing what I did.'

'That makes two of us, kid. But being sorry about what we did in the past won't help either of us. We need to focus on the here and now, and on doing our best to get the job done.'

The cab slowed to a halt outside what appeared to be a disused industrial building on a poorly lit Soho back street.

'Okay, this is it,' Perry said.

He paid the driver and we stepped out into the night

air, which suddenly felt much cooler than it had when we had left the hotel less than half an hour earlier. I looked up and down the street as the cab performed a U-turn and headed back towards the main road, and what I saw didn't exactly inspire me with confidence. There wasn't another person in sight, let alone the throngs of people that you'd normally expect to see milling around a club. On the contrary, this was a dark, silent and unappealing place, and the windows of the monstrous black-bricked building that we had come to visit looked as if they had been boarded up—and graffitied over—decades ago.

'Are you sure that this is it?' I asked. 'It looks pretty dead to me.'

Perry walked past the front of the building and then took a sharp left into a narrow alleyway that I hadn't even noticed was there. Not wanting to lose sight of him for too long, I quickly followed, but by the time I had turned the corner he had already reached the end of the alley, and was waiting for me in front of a heavy black door. He grabbed the handle and then paused until I had caught up with him.

'Make sure you stay close, and don't talk to anyone,' he said. 'Got that?'

I looked around to see if I'd missed something, but there still wasn't anyone around to talk to. 'Sure,' I said, shrugging my agreement.

'Good.'

He turned back to face the door, took a deep breath, as if steeling himself for something terrible, and opened it.

CHAPTER SIXTEEN

The moment Perry opened the heavy black door, we were hit by a wave of loud heavy metal music, and the whole building seemed to transform into a completely different place. When I followed him inside, I found myself in a large room full of bizarrely costumed patrons. Some were sitting around upended barrels which served as rudimentary tables, others were standing at a bar that ran the length of the room at the back, and a few were simply standing in small groups. Every person I could see here was unusual in some respect. There were nuns wearing extremely short leather habits and suitably holey fishnet stockings, goatee-bearded men wearing horns and black suits, and about a dozen others with skin so pale and faces so gaunt that they could have come straight from the set of a zombie movie.

When Perry had described Hell as a club, I'd imagined something a bit more upmarket than one that used barrels for tables, but this place was as seedy as they came, which says a lot when you consider that we were in Soho. The floor was a seamless slab of concrete, covered with a thin layer of dirty grey sawdust, and a spacious grid of wide iron girders served as the ceiling. Hanging from those girders were three giant metal cages, each of which contained a naked girl dancing. I use the word dancing rather loosely, because all they were really doing was holding onto the cage bars and gyrating up and down for the benefit of the people standing below. One of those people was me, and in a moment of very ungentlemanly reflection I wondered why the ceiling in the bedroom of my Brighton home couldn't have a crack like that.

Catching myself thinking such things whilst on a mission to rescue my soul mate, and fearing that I might go blind or something, I tore my eyes away from the dancer above and took a deep breath to calm myself. The air was hot—uncomfortably so—and thick with the heady aroma of beer and sex. A bit like a Wetherspoons after dark.

I scanned the whole room and I couldn't see anyone who looked even remotely normal until a refreshingly flesh-coloured girl in a red latex leotard approached me with a big smile and even bigger breasts.

'Hey you, what's up?' she said, and without waiting for an answer she reached down to grab my crotch.

It was the kind of move that I'd always wished a woman would make on me, but something instinctive caused me to take a step back.

'Not that,' Perry told her, and he quickly dragged me away.

The woman hissed at him angrily, then blew me a kiss and turned her attention to a guy with so many piercings in his face that he made Pinhead look decidedly smooth.

The metal face grinned when she grabbed his crotch in a similar manner, and a moment later she was leading him towards a secluded booth area in the far corner.

'It's like a night out in the rough part of Brighton,' I said as another completely naked woman stepped onto a raised stage area and started moving pornographically around a pole.

'Except that this isn't just fancy dress,' Perry said. 'These guys really are demons.'

To be honest, I couldn't really tell the difference, but I did notice that people seemed to be watching us closely as we walked through the club towards the bar. I nodded politely and forced a smile whenever I was unlucky enough to make direct eye contact with anyone, but all I got back were cold stares and one guy who thought it necessary to take a ridiculously large hunting knife out of his pocket and start using the tip of the blade to clean his fingernails in an overtly threatening manner.

'Where's your boss?' Perry asked when we finally reached the bar. His question was aimed at the barman, who was a slimy looking guy with slicked-back hair. He was wearing a fishnet vest that allowed two rusted-nail nipple piercings to poke through. Self-mutilation was clearly quite popular around here.

'He's out,' the barman said,

'Bullshit.'

The barman bared his teeth, which were as fanged as any you'd see on a fully grown Rottweiler, and growled. It was a low, rumbling growl, and really not the kind of sound that I would have expected any human being to make unless they were leaning over a gutter after imbibing half a dozen cans of Special Brew.

Perry wasn't fazed by the sound. 'Look,' he said, 'I don't have time to trade unpleasantries with you, so just go and tell him that he has a visitor, okay?'

The barman didn't budge. He just stood there, his teeth still bared.

'Okay,' Perry sniffed. 'I understand that you have a job to do, so why don't I just give you my calling card instead?'

He reached into the inside pocket of his jacket, pulled something out and put the back of his clenched fist on the bar. Then, slowly and deliberately, he opened his hand to reveal a small ball of something that was glowing white. Impossibly white. So white that it illuminated the whole room. Weirdly, the ball wasn't actually resting on his palm, but appeared to be levitating about an inch above it.

The response in the club was immediate. The music stopped, the dancers froze, the chattering ceased and the barman stepped back, his eyes wide with fear. All of a sudden, the intimidating Rottweiler of a moment ago had been transformed into a shivering Chihuahua.

Perry stared at the barman for a long moment, then slowly looked around the room and smiled. He closed his fist around the ball and put it back in his pocket. The illumination of a few seconds ago was now gone, and the club had returned to looking just as dark and dingy as it had when we'd entered, but the tension in the place hadn't eased one bit.

'Alright,' the barman said, slowly regaining his composure. 'Wait here.'

I watched as he turned and disappeared through a back door, then I looked at Perry, my mind still trying to figure out whatever it was that I had just witnessed. 'What was that?'

'Light,' Perry said, his tone hushed. 'The kind that destroys demons on impact.'

He glanced around at everyone else in the bar. All eyes were on us, and when he looked at the demons, they hissed in unison, like a den of vipers.

'Even Salt?'

Perry shrugged. 'I'm not sure if it would actually destroy him like it does the others, but it would certainly put him out of commission for a while.'

'Then why didn't you use it before?' I asked. 'Back at my place, when you were getting seven bells of shit kicked out of you, for example? Or at Natalie's hotel, instead of letting us just stand there and get gaffer-taped like a bloody Christmas present?'

He leaned in, bowed his head and lowered his voice even more. 'Because I can only use it once,' he said. 'And any human who happens to be within a metre of the thing when it goes off, gets destroyed. No, not destroyed, that's not a strong enough word. They get spiritually obliterated, as if they'd never existed in the first place. And that doesn't make it the ideal weapon for close-range confrontations.'

'So it's just for show.'

'It's a last resort, for life-and-death situations only. Like a cyanide pill. The only thing for show around here is the condom you've had in your wallet for the last three years.'

'Very funny.'

Perry grinned, and he might well have added something else to his oh-so-hilarious jibe, but then the back door opened and Doran Salt entered, closely followed by the barman. Salt looked serious, but not particularly intimidated.

'You escaped faster than I expected,' he said.

'We're full of surprises,' Perry told him. 'Where are the girls?'

'They're quite safe. I have Vinnie taking care of their every need as we speak.'

'I want to see them. Now.'

'Then why didn't you just say so?' Salt turned and started back towards the door. 'Show them through,' he told the barman as he left.

The Rottweiler-turned-Chihuahua nodded and obediently opened a hatch in the bar, then stepped aside and motioned for us to go into the back room. I glanced at Perry, half-wondering if this might not be some kind of trap, but I figured that he knew a lot more about Satanic shenanigans than I did, so I said nothing and waited for him to respond. He shot me his own look of suspicion—one that I took as a silent warning to be wary —before walking through the hatch and following after Salt.

Natalie and Jenny were sitting on a couple of old wooden chairs when we arrived, and were being watched over by Vinnie, who was standing in the middle of the room with his arms folded across his chest. The girls jumped from their seats the moment they laid eyes on us. Natalie hugged me tighter than any female had ever hugged me in my entire life, and Jenny gave Perry an equally enthusiastic welcome.

Having Natalie in my arms like this made me realise just how much I'd been worrying about her welfare.

'Thank God you're okay,' I said. 'I really didn't know that any of this was going to happen.'

'Stop.' She looked up at me, smiled, and hugged me even tighter. 'I'm just glad that you're safe too. We were worried about you. About both of you.'

'Alright, that's enough of the Harlequin Romance nonsense,' Salt said. 'The exit is that way.' He pointed back to the door.

'We're not going anywhere without the girls,' Perry said.

'So take them with you.'

Perry narrowed his eyes. 'What, you're just going to let us walk out of here?'

He glanced over at me, and I could tell that he was wondering the same thing that I was: Why the hell would Salt kidnap them and then let them go without even attempting to put up a fight?

'I've been told that you've brought Light into this place.'

Now Perry understood, and he straightened up. Braver. More confident. 'That's right,' he said. He reached into his inside pocket, and then paused. 'Do you want some?'

Salt glared at him. 'No, that won't be necessary. Just take what you came for and leave.'

Perry removed his hand from his jacket, leaving the Light in his pocket, and patted it gently. 'Nice doing business with you.' He turned to me and nodded towards the door. 'Come on. Let's get out of here before we catch something.'

We headed out of the room the way we had entered, all the while keeping a careful eye on Salt and Vinnie, just in case they had any plans to do something the moment our backs were turned. Fortunately for us, they both stood perfectly still, watching us closely but not making any effort to prevent us from leaving. It was a similar situation in the bar, but there the demons actually stepped out of our way as we walked across the still-silent room towards the exit.

The sense of relief that we felt when we finally emerged from the building was palpable. Natalie hugged me tight once more, this time kissing me on the cheek as she did so, and then she went over to embrace Perry and Jenny. The two girls started reassuring each other that everything was going to be fine now, and I took the opportunity to sidle up to Perry.

'She kissed me on the cheek.'

'I saw,' he said. 'But that doesn't count. She needs to kiss you because she loves you, and not just because she's relieved that she's still alive.'

I looked back at her and thought about going over to get yet another hug. Maybe the third time would prove to be the luckiest.

'Not yet,' Perry said, as if reading my mind. 'Right now we need to get as far away from this place as we can. Salt's up to something, I can feel it, and I don't want to stick around to find out what it is.'

CHAPTER SEVENTEEN

The cab ride back to Natalie's hotel was without incident, and the two girls seemed to be in remarkably high spirits, chatting amongst themselves about nothing in particular and occasionally giggling over shared jokes. Their jovial mood was probably understandable, given the ordeal that they had been through and the fact that they were now free once more, but Perry and I were feeling rather more reserved. Yes, we'd managed to liberate Natalie and Jenny from Salt's clutches, which was fantastic, but the whole episode had wasted valuable time. There were less than twenty-four hours to go before the impending dissolution of the universe, and I still had quite a way to go to complete my mission. My only consolation was that Natalie didn't seem to be blaming me for the whole kidnapping thing with Salt. In fact, she hadn't even mentioned it.

The girls were still buzzing when we entered their suite at the hotel. Natalie made straight for the king-sized bed in her room and flopped onto it.

'God, I love this room,' she said.

Perry shot me a confused glance, then shook his head. 'Look,' he said. 'Maybe we should explain what happened tonight.'

'No need,' Jenny said. 'We've figured it out already.'

'You have?' I asked, not even trying to conceal my surprise.

Natalie sat up. 'That's right, Mr Fenton. You just want to get inside my panties.' She flopped back down onto the bed, giggling like an adolescent schoolgirl.

'What?'

Jenny pointed at me and laughed. 'Look, he's blushing.'

'That's because he's a naughty boy with a dirty mind,' Natalie quipped.

'No,' I said. 'It's because it's not true.'

Natalie sat up again, but this time only half of the way, so that she could rest on her elbows. 'You mean you don't want to get inside my panties?' She pouted, as if sadly disappointed by the idea.

'Have you been drinking?' Perry asked.

'Only a glass or two,' she said.

'Three or four, more like,' Jenny corrected with a grin. 'Mr Salt has the finest Champagne I've ever tasted.'

Perry rolled his eyes. 'Well, I think that you've both had just a little too much. And it's been a long and eventful evening, so you should both probably get some sleep.'

'Nonsense,' Jenny said, a sudden scowl on her face making her grin a distant memory. 'It's only...' She checked her watch. 'Two-thirty.'

'Yeah, but that's two-thirty in the morning,' I reminded her.

'Perfect!' Natalie said, and she jumped up to her feet. 'We should go out!'

'What do you mean, go out?' I asked. 'We've only just got back in.'

'But out is better,' Jenny said. 'Where to, Nat?'

'Dancing. At a jazz club, maybe. There's a lovely little place no more than ten minutes from here.' She lowered her head slightly and rolled her eyes up at me, clearly aware of how to look deliberately seductive when she wanted to. 'It's very intimate.'

I know that it probably wasn't appropriate, given the gravity of the situation that we were all in, but the way she said those three words caused something to stir in my jockey shorts, and I felt my face flush slightly.

Jenny stood up, grabbed Natalie by the wrist and led her friend into the *en suite* bathroom before closing the door behind them. Perry stared at the door for several seconds, and I don't think that either one of us could quite grasp what was happening.

'This is a bit weird, isn't it?' I asked the question quietly so that the girls wouldn't be able to overhear. 'Their reaction to tonight, I mean.'

He nodded. 'Looks like Salt gave them more than Champagne, that's for sure.'

'You think he slipped something into their drinks?'

'It wouldn't be the first time he's done something like that.'

'And do you really think they know anything?'

'About what?'

'About the mission. They said they'd figured out what we were up to. Maybe Salt told them.'

'We can't assume that,' he said. 'But the fact that they think they know what's going on works in our favour.'

'It does? Why?'

'Because it means that we don't have to cover things up. Whether they know about the mission itself, or they just think that you want to get into her panties, you have the same opportunity to get close and pull this thing off.'

'Only if I'm quick about it. We only have one day left.'

'Which is why we'd be wise to make the most of tonight, and take them to the jazz club.'

I shook my head. 'No way. I couldn't dance if my life depended on it.'

'Your life does depend on it, and so does mine,' Perry said. 'So you're dancing. Just think Cary Grant and try not to tread on her toes too often.'

I was about to protest and tell him that my talent for dancing was as lacking as my talent for splitting the atom, but as soon as I opened my mouth to speak, the girls emerged from the bathroom. They were giggling for no apparent reason, and both of them looked far too bright and sparkly for the lateness of the hour. Maybe Perry was right, and they were high on something that Salt had added to their drinks. In which case, would an intoxicated kiss from Natalie be enough to save the world, or would I have to wait for her to sober up before I could seal the deal? Somehow, I couldn't imagine that proving my blatant lack of ability on a dance floor would lead to a kiss of any description, so maybe the question was redundant to begin with.

The jazz club was a retro-looking place of dark mahogany and burgundy trimmings that would have made it seem like night no matter what the hour. It was fairly empty, which wasn't a complete surprise, given the time, but music was still being played and the barman—thankfully, a very normal-looking human being wearing a white shirt, silver tie and grey waistcoat—was perfectly happy to serve us drinks. Natalie and Jenny both chose Sea Breeze cocktails (which comprised vodka and fruit juice, as far as I could tell), Perry ordered a soda water and I, after looking at the drinks menu and finding nothing that sounded remotely like my usual pint of bitter, settled for a Martini. You know by now that I'm not really a Martini kind of bloke, but if it was good enough for James Bond, it was probably good enough for me, and it came in the kind of glass that I'm sure even Cary Grant would have been happy with.

We took our seats at a candlelit table on the edge of the dance floor and made small talk for a while, casually commenting on the decor, the drinks, and how nice it was that we had the place all to ourselves. Then Perry asked Jenny if she'd like to 'trip the light fantastic'. She replied by saying that she would be delighted, and a few seconds later they were both gliding around the dance floor like they'd been doing it for years. I thought the whole 'light fantastic' approach was ridiculously cheesy, but Jenny seemed to have lapped it up, confirming once again Perry's statement about old-fashioned manners never getting old. He caught me watching them and nodded for me to turn my attention back to Natalie, which I promptly did.

'I'm really sorry about all of this,' I said.

'All of what?'

'You were kidnapped, remember?'

'Oh, that.'

She looked over at Perry and Jenny on the dance floor and smiled, but I wasn't going to let the conversation die out quite that soon.

'Yes, that. Well, as I said, I really am sorry.'

'Why are you sorry?' she asked. 'You didn't kidnap me.'

'I know, but I still feel guilty. I mean, it was my idea to take you to dinner and... God, I've screwed things up big time, haven't I?'

She didn't respond. In fact, I wasn't even sure that she was listening to me, because she seemed to be far more interested in watching the fancy footwork of our chaperones. She'd been as enthusiastic as a hippie in a hemp factory when we were all back at the hotel, but now she didn't even appear to be environmentally friendly. If Salt really had spiked her drinks back at the Hell club then the effects were clearly beginning to wear off.

Maybe I had already blown it. Maybe the events that had followed our romantic dinner for two had given her cause to back off a bit. Maybe I was so crap with women that I was now getting friend-zoned even by my divinely appointed soul mate. Here I was, with the most gorgeous woman I'd ever met, and she was slipping through my fingers.

I needed to do something to salvage my chances, and fast.

Come on, Fenton. Think.

What would Cary Grant do?

He'd say something romantic, stupid.

'Okay,' I said, as much to the voice in my head as to

Natalie. 'Let me get right to the point because time isn't on my side here. I'm fully aware of the fact that we've only just met, but I think—no, I know—that we have some kind of connection. Under normal circumstances I'd try to be patient and let things develop at their own pace, but my circumstances aren't exactly normal. I can't say any more than that right now, but I need to ask you... do you feel the same way?'

Again, she didn't respond. Her eyes remained fixed on Perry and Jenny.

'Or anything similar?' I asked. 'At all?'

Finally, she turned to me and smiled.

'We should dance,' she said. And with that, she stood up, grabbed my hand and pulled me onto the dance floor.

Now, I don't quite know how I had expected Natalie to respond to my heartfelt confession that I was harbouring warm and fuzzy feelings for her, but I was pretty sure that Cary Grant would have fared better. Had this been a movie, my soul mate would have swooned on the spot, leaned in for the kiss to end all kisses and we would have proceeded to live happily ever after. In addition, the universe would have been saved and Doran Salt would have been banished back to whatever putrid pit of fiery bollocks he had come from.

Instead of all that, I found myself standing like a soggy washcloth in the middle of the dance floor, my left hand holding Natalie's right, and my right hand resting politely on her waist. Adopting the proper position for slow dancing was easy enough, but actually doing it was something else entirely, and I had to keep a very close eye on how Perry was shifting his feet to get the hang of moving in sync with my own partner. Fortunately for me, Natalie seemed to be in a world of her own, and completely unaware of the efforts that I was making to try and conceal my severe lack of ability. When she leaned in and rested her head on my shoulder, the wave of relaxation that I felt was almost palpable. Dancing this close was much easier, because it wasn't so much dancing as simply swaying back and forth in time with the music.

As we stood there, swaying, I passed the time by continuing to watch Perry and Jenny. They were also dancing close, but their embrace looked to be even more intimate. He had both of his hands on her hips, whilst she had hers clasped around the back of his neck. They were staring into each other's eyes like young lovers, and they were having a conversation about something, but I wasn't quite close enough to make out their words. After a couple of minutes of straining to hear what they were saying, I allowed my curiosity to get the better of me, and I discreetly swayed Natalie across the dance floor until I was within eavesdropping distance.

'You know what I want, Perry?' Jenny had virtually breathed the question into his ear.

'No, but I have a feeling that you're about to tell me.'

'You're right, I am.' She mashed her body up against his. 'I want you to take me back to my hotel room, throw me down on the bed and fuck my pretty little brains out.'

Now, I'm no prude, as my one-time subscription to Creamed Leaks magazine should verify, but I was genuinely surprised by Jenny's forthright comment, which left absolutely nothing to the imagination.

'Is that right?' Perry grinned broadly.

She nodded, slowly and seductively. 'Mh-hmm. So will you do that for me, Perry?'

Perry looked at her, and for a second I could have sworn that his face had reddened a little, as if the old man was actually blushing. Jenny didn't appear to notice, and so she continued with her verbal assault on his nobler aspirations, which would, I felt, soon fall off one by one.

'Will you fuck me long and hard until I squeal?'

Now he stopped dancing, or swaying, or however you want to describe the thing that he'd been doing, and he took a step back.

'Squeal?' he said.

She looked up at him, his eyes widened a fraction and all of a sudden his grin had vanished.

'Excuse me,' he said, 'but I need to pay a visit to the big boy's room.'

'My, my, aren't you the modest one?' she giggled.

He smiled politely at her, then came over to me, grabbed me by the jacket and pulled me towards the rest room at the back of the club. Natalie was momentarily surprised to find herself dancing alone, but she soon found Jenny and they quickly took to swaying with each other instead.

'Can I just say that I tend to get a bit annoyed with people who drag me around like a rag doll?'

'Just shut up and act normal,' Perry said, and without even attempting to provide any explanation for his actions he pushed me unceremoniously through the door marked Cool Cats.

Whilst the men's room at the jazz club was bright, clean and stylish in a white-splashed-with-mahogany-motifs kind of way, it occurred to me that I was beginning to spend far too much time in these places. 'Do we always need to swap notes in rooms that have urinals hanging on the wall?' I asked.

'This is important.'

'Well, it had better be, because the girls are all over us out there.'

Perry shook his head. 'No, they aren't.'

I waited for the punchline, but there was no humour in his eyes. Just a serious look of grave concern.

'What are you on about? Jenny was pressing up against you so hard she almost popped her implants.'

He flared his nostrils, clearly pissed about something, but took a deep breath to calm himself. 'That isn't Jenny.'

Had he not been drinking soda water, I would have suspected that he'd had one too many. 'Look, mate... Are you feeling alright?'

'It's a demon.'

Laugh? I nearly pissed myself, which would have been ironic in a room which was specifically designed to prevent such an embarrassment.

Perry scowled at me. 'Natalie, too.'

I stopped laughing. 'You're serious.'

'Yeah.'

'But how can you tell?'

'Jenny has hell in her eyes.'

'What does that even mean?'

'It's a demon thing,' he said. 'They can hide their true nature for a certain length of time, but not forever.'

'A bit like a Scouser, then.'

Perry didn't respond to my feeble attempt to lighten the mood, and continued as if he hadn't even heard it. 'Sooner or later they let the facade slip and you can see what's underneath.'

'And what did you see underneath, with Jenny?'

'I saw the fire of hell in her eyes.'

I couldn't really imagine what the fire of hell might have looked like, or how it might differ—if at all—from the bright orange glow of an industrial furnace, but I wasn't about to press him for more details.

And then the penny dropped.

'Hang on,' I said. 'If those girls out there are demons, then that means—'

Perry nodded. 'The real Natalie and Jenny are still with Salt.'

The realisation was like a punch in the gut from a really big bloke with anvils for fists. 'Oh,' I said, suddenly feeling the need to lean back against the hand dryer on the wall.

'Yeah.' He shook his head regretfully. 'I should have known. Salt didn't put up any kind of fight when we went to get the girls. In fact he couldn't get rid of them quick enough.'

'I assumed that was because of the Light thing.'

'You and me both, kid.' He frowned and shook his head again, then took a deep breath and straightened up. 'But we don't have time to dwell on that. We need to get out of here. Those things on the dance floor have probably been ordered to keep us away from the girls at all costs, so it won't be easy.'

'Well, they don't know that we know, do they?'

'So?'

'So can't we just go along with it for a few more minutes?'

He shrugged. 'And then what?'

'I don't know,' I admitted. 'Make our excuses and take them back to their hotel? Or just do a runner?'

Perry mulled the idea over for a few moments, and then nodded. 'Okay. But try to act normal. If they figure out that we're onto them, we'll be in even deeper shit than we are already.'

His response was encouraging. For once in my life, I had come up with a plan of action to try and solve a problem instead of simply moaning about it. Feeling rather empowered by my new-found sense of initiative, I stood upright, pulled my shoulders back and nodded for him to open the door so that we could head back to the dance floor.

He took hold of the door and opened it slowly, just a few inches, before leaning closer to peek out through the gap. As if waiting for her cue, Jenny's face appeared right in front of him. Her eyes were burning orange, like transparent globes of fire, and her grin now revealed a danger-ous-looking set of sharp fanged teeth.

'Hey Perry,' she giggled. Her voice still sounded like Jenny's, but it now had an underlying hiss of hatred.

He turned and looked at me. 'Well, good luck, kid,' he said, but that was all that he could manage before Jenny pushed the door open wider to reveal an equally demonic-looking Natalie standing alongside her.

The girls snarled threateningly.

CHAPTER EIGHTEEN

There were lots of useful things that I had learned by this point in my life. For example, the reassurance that 'it's in the post' actually means that it most definitely isn't, and that, by the time you can confirm the fact, it will be too late for you to do anything about it. Similarly, whenever you get a phone call and the person on the other end of the line opens the conversation by assuring you that they are 'definitely not calling to sell you anything' then they are most definitely calling to sell you something, and it's invariably something that you absolutely do not need.

Politicians are self-serving slimeballs no matter where they happen to be positioned on the political spectrum, mixing your drinks is never a good idea, New Year resolutions are far easier to set than they are to stick to, things always cost more than you expect, talk is cheap, size does matter, at least half of all blondes were born brunette, nine out of ten statistical statements are made up on the spot, and nothing lasts forever.

As I said, life had helped me to learn many useful

things, but one thing that it hadn't taught me was how to handle being cornered in a men's bathroom by two snarling demons in evening dresses. Unfortunately, that was precisely the situation that I now found myself in, so I was fairly tense, as you can imagine. So tense, in fact, that my anus felt like it was inhaling the fabric of my jockey shorts like a black hole sucking in space debris. I apologise for that rather graphic description, but I really do think that I have a duty to convey the severity of the situation.

Now, if I'd been a braver soul, I might have risen to the occasion by straightening my stance, cracking my neck from side to side and saying 'Bring it on' in my very best Batman voice. But I wasn't a braver soul, I was just me, and so I didn't do any of that. Instead, I decided to try and handle the situation a bit more creatively.

'There's no need to snarl, ladies,' I said in as calm a tone as I could muster. 'So what if you're a couple of demons? You still look pretty hot to me, so why can't we just carry on where we left off and have some fun?'

Perry turned to look at me, his jaw slack. 'What the—'

'Don't mind my friend here,' I said, cutting him short. 'He wouldn't know a good thing if it kicked him in the bollocks and bent down to kiss them better. But me...' I stepped closer to the door so that I was standing just a foot or two away from the two snarlers. 'I'm a man of the world. And, to be honest, I don't really buy into this whole 'mission from God' crap. In fact, I really don't give a shit about who runs the universe. Right now, I just want to get laid.'

The demon girls looked at me, then at each other, and then back at me. 'Which one of us do you want?' asked the one that looked like Natalie. She was licking her lips and grinning her fangy grin. There would be no blow jobs required from that one tonight, that was for sure.

'Why make me choose?' was my smooth response. 'Can't I have both of you?' I nodded towards the area behind them. 'Can't all three of us get nasty out there? There's plenty of room.'

The two of them turned in unison to look wantonly at the dance floor, and the moment they did, I made my move, surging forward with my forearms crossed in front of me and charging through them like an American footballer. Both demons were caught off balance and stumbled to the floor. They snarled and started scrambling to get back to their feet, but Perry kept them down by using them as stepping stones as he followed me out.

To say that I was feeling a tad pleased with myself at this point would be akin to saying that the Pope can sometimes be a bit religious, and I flashed a self-satisfied grin at the agent. 'Are we Cool Cats, or are we Cool Cats?'

'You're a frickin' genius,' Perry said. 'But let's hold back on the celebrations until we're actually outta this place, yeah?'

He had a point. The girls from hell had almost recovered from their trip, and although I knew very little about the demonic fraternity, it was a fair bet that, if they got to us before we got to the exit, we'd be royally buggered, and not in the blue-blooded-erotica sense of the phrase. Fortunately, we were now just a dozen or so paces from the exit, so the chances of them being able to catch up with us were slim.

Or so I thought.

I managed to take only two more steps in the right

direction before I noticed the barman standing in front of the main doors. This was the same friendly barman who had served us our drinks only half an hour earlier, but now he had a deranged look in his eyes. He was also armed for a fight, with a knife in his right hand and half a lemon in his left.

Looking back over my shoulder, I saw that Perry was running towards me. Both of the demon girls were pursuing him, growling and gnashing their teeth like rabid animals, so turning back wasn't an option.

'Keep going,' Perry said as he approached.

'We can't. The exit's blocked.'

'Not for long,' he said, and he continued running straight past me and directly into the path of the barman.

I braced myself to witness a horrible impact—the kind that would make Perry one with the knife blade, like a spiritually enlightened kebab—but it didn't happen. Instead, he span around at the very last second, kicking both the knife and the half-lemon out of the barman's hands. The knife landed several feet away, and as the barman watched it skid across the floor, Perry snatched the half-lemon out of the air and deftly squeezed its juice into the eyes of his opponent. The demon barman screamed in agony and crumpled to the floor. His head met the ground with a thud, rendering him usefully unconscious.

Had the barman been our only foe, our sticky situation would have been resolved right there and then, but we still had the two demon girls to contend with.

'Use the Light,' I told Perry.

He shook his head. 'Not unless it's absolutely necessary.'

'How much more necessary can it get?'

He wasn't listening, but was already off in pursuit of the discarded knife, so I decided to take matters into my own hands for a second time by dashing over to the bar. I opened the wooden hatch to allow myself entrance, closed it behind me, grabbed a handful of lemons from a box underneath the counter and scrambled around, looking for a spare knife. I eventually found one in a drawer and quickly started cutting the lemons in half.

'What the hell are you doing?' Perry asked when he finally caught up with me. By this time, the demon girls had taken a quick look at the crumpled barman, snarled at each other and were once again heading in our direction. They had looked pretty angry even before seeing their comrade knocked out of commission, but now they were positively livid.

'What does it look like? I'm getting more lemons ready.' I sliced through a fourth and added the two halves to a growing yellow pile.

'For what?'

'Well, you used the juice against the barman, and he went down like a sack of potatoes. So it's obviously some kind of demon thing. A weakness. Right?'

'No, you idiot. It was a fluky lemon juice thing. I was desperate and that was all I had.'

In my defence, I really hadn't had much time to think things through properly, but I had to admit that his explanation did make a bit more sense than mine. Unfortunately, my actions meant that I had now trapped myself behind the bar, and the demon that looked like Natalie was already opening the wooden hatch to join me. Perry would probably have been willing to help me out, but the

Jenny demon was now lunging at him with vicious-looking fingernails, and he was backing off quickly in the opposite direction.

For the moment, at least, I was on my own.

I looked around for something to defend myself with, but the closest thing to me was the knife in my hand and the pile of halved lemons on the bar itself. The Natalie demon stepped through the opening and cornered me, her eyes blazing fiercely, so I made an attempt to replicate Perry's fluke by taking a lemon and squeezing it as hard as I could.

Note to self: The next time you do something stupid like that, please remember to point the cut half of the lemon in the right direction.

The juice in my eyes blinded me for a second, so I did the only thing I could, and backed away. I felt around for another lemon, but instead found an open jar of maraschino cherries, and I quickly started throwing them at the demon one by one, as if they were miniature red grenades. They didn't do much damage, of course, but the assault did buy me the few precious seconds that I needed to hop onto the bar and over the other side. Only then did I notice that I'd ditched a perfectly good knife in order to wage war with a jar of cherries, and I kicked myself for my blatant lack of initiative. I'd seen First Blood a dozen times, yet I'd set aside a perfectly dangerous weapon in favour of preserved fruit. John Rambo would not have been impressed.

'I could use some help here, pal.'

Perry was in trouble. He was sprawled on the floor, and Jenny was standing over him, her hands raised like claws, as if she were a big cat getting ready to pounce.

'Not so fast, Buttercup.'

I ran over to apprehend her, only vaguely wondering why I had called her Buttercup, but she turned to snarl at me instead and I stopped in my tracks. Perry wisely used the moment or two afforded by this distraction to get back to his feet, but her eyes were fixed on me now, and as far as I was concerned that wasn't really a much better outcome.

Now I stood, frozen to the spot, and swallowed hard. I knew that the demon girls wanted rid of me, but how would they achieve it? Perry had already told me that I couldn't be attacked directly, so what were they going to do? Follow me around and snarl me to death? And how would that work? Wasn't I already dead? Or did I still count as being alive for matter-of-life-and-death purposes?

By the time I had finished ruminating over these questions, Perry was standing directly behind the Jenny demon.

He tapped her on the shoulder. 'Hey, you forgot this.'

She turned, and just as she did so, he pulled his fist back, and then unleashed an almighty punch. I know it was almighty because the demon somehow anticipated the move and swiftly dodged to the right, leaving the path clear for Perry's clenched fist to smack me directly in the face.

'Oh, jeez.' He winced at the own goal. 'I'm sorry, pal.'

I swore into the palms of my hands, carefully feeling the bridge of my nose with my fingertips to see if it was broken. Nothing wobbled, but it hurt like a really hurty bastard of a thing, and I cursed the moment in which

Perry Barr had stepped into my previously mundane—but far less physically painful—life.

The demon Jenny was laughing at my obvious discomfort, and Perry took advantage of the moment by sweeping the back of her knees Bruce Lee style and sending her crashing to the ground. Then he reached out, grabbed my arm and pulled me to one side. A half-empty Jack Daniels bottle missed my head by the merest whisker, and when I turned to see where it had come from, I saw the demonic Natalie still holding onto it. She looked surprised that her swing of the blunt instrument had missed its mark.

Not wanting to stick around just to find out how she would respond, we ran back towards the main door, smiled at the fact that the barman was still out for the count, and finally managed to reach the exit.

'Good going, kid,' Perry said as he reached out to pull the door open, but then he looked back at me, alarmed. 'It's locked.'

'How the hell can it be locked?' I gave the handle a good tug myself, just in case he was suddenly being old and feeble. Then I tried pushing the door open, just in case I was suddenly being young and backward. The door didn't budge either way. 'It wasn't locked earlier. Maybe the barman used some kind of demonic curse to seal us in.'

Perry glared at me. 'Seriously? That's the most likely thing you can think of?' He didn't wait for a response, but instead looked over at the barman on the floor. 'There,' he said, then ran over to the unconscious figure, unclipped a bunch of keys from his belt, and returned.

There was nothing I could say to excuse my shameful

lack of common sense, but the agent was in too much of a rush to make a big deal of it. He quickly started trying each key in the door in an effort to find the one that would unlock it.

The girls were snarling once more. They had gathered themselves together and were now embarking on yet another wave of attack, whilst also taking it in turns to swig from the bottle of Jack Daniels as they staggered in our direction.

'Quick, they're coming again.' I said. 'They're unstoppable. It's like a drunken zombie apocalypse, or something. Use the Light while you still can.'

He shook his head. 'We might need it even more when we get out of here. Besides, there aren't many more to try. Have faith.'

The demonic Natalie was eyeing me like a cat would eye a cornered mouse, and I estimated that if we didn't get out in the next sixty seconds, we wouldn't survive to see a sixty-first.

'The Light, Perry! I don't do faith!'

The moment I uttered those words, the locking mechanism of the main door clicked free.

'Well, that's a real shame,' Perry said with a told-you-so tone that pissed me off royally, and he pulled the door open.

We tumbled out of the club as fast as we could and closed the door behind us with only moments to spare. There was an angry thump as the lunging claws of the pursuing demons hit the wooden barrier, followed by screeches of fury. Perry had wisely kept the appropriate key at the ready and had soon managed to lock the girls inside.

'That might hold them for a couple of minutes, but not much longer,' he said.

I nodded. I still thought that the whole ordeal would have been much easier to handle if he'd used the Light thing in his jacket pocket, but he was clearly a stubborn old goat when he wanted to be, and I no longer had any energy left to argue my case.

'So, what now?' I asked. The streets outside the jazz club were empty, and whilst I appreciated the complete absence of demons out here, I was keen for us to get as far away as possible from the two that we had left inside. And quick.

'I don't know.'

'What do you mean, you don't know?'

'What I mean is that, right now, I'm as clueless as you are.'

'We can't both be clueless!' I protested, albeit quite irrationally. Of course we could both be clueless. In fact, our current and complete lack of clues was demonstrating not only the possibility of that situation, but the reality of it. What I meant was: 'We don't have time!'

Perry shook his head, in much the same way as a father might shake his head at an impatient toddler. 'Haven't you learned anything yet? We might not have a clue, and we might not have much time, but we have what's important.'

'Which is?'

'Faith.'

I rolled my eyes. The problem with spiritual people is that they get so used to denying reality that they simply aren't capable of recognising when they're up Shit Creek without a paddle. I reached into my pocket and removed my phone, then launched my *Jab-a-Cab* application and waited for it to log me in. 'We need more than faith to get a taxi out here in the next few minutes. Especially at this time of night. We need a fucking miracle.'

And, right on cue, the miracle appeared in the form of a white convertible sports car with the top down that tore around the corner and screeched to a halt in front of us. A dark-skinned guy wearing a white suit and aviator-style sunglasses was grinning exuberantly at us from the driver's seat. He looked familiar, but I couldn't quite place him until he raised his sunglasses—which I assumed he was wearing purely for aesthetic purposes, given that the sun wouldn't even begin to rise for another couple of hours—and rested them on his head.

'Amit?'

'Who?' Perry asked.

'Good to see you, my friend,' Amit said, the grin still wide on his face. 'And I am very pleased to be making your acquaintance too, Mister Barr.'

Perry looked even more confused now that the driver had seemed to know who he was without having been introduced.

'We shared a holding cell in the afterlife,' I explained. 'Just before God gave me a piece of her mind.'

'So you're the backup...' Perry said, smiling.

'Precisely!' Amit said. 'My mission is to help you find the girls so that you may succeed in your quest.'

Snarls of rage were being snarled inside the jazz club.

'But what about the pussy?' I asked, remembering his ambition to be reborn as a bad case of genital warts.

'If you do not succeed in your quest then there will be no pussy for anyone, so you had better get in, and fast.'

Perry appeared surprised both by my question and by Amit's response, but he didn't waste time pursuing it. Instead, he walked around the car and got into the passenger seat, leaving me no option but to cram myself into the paltry excuse for a back seat, which turned out to be even less accommodating than it looked.

'How come you get to sit in the front?' I asked the agent.

'Because it's a company car, and I'm with the company.'

It was a fair point, so I didn't argue. What I did do was tap Amit on the shoulder. 'Do you know how to get to Hell?'

'Of course,' he said. 'I am no shit for brains.' He brought his sunglasses back down into position. 'Now, enough with the questions. We have a mission to complete.'

And with that, he slammed his foot down on the accelerator and we were on our way, leaving behind two extremely pissed-off demon girls and the smell of burning rubber.

CHAPTER NINETEEN

Amit tore though the streets of London as if he'd been cast to play the leading role in the latest Fast and Furious movie, screeching around corners at high speed, racing to beat the traffic lights at every opportunity and generally doing whatever was necessary to throw me around the back seat like a cramped sack of potatoes.

I didn't complain about the ride because, after the ordeal of the jazz club, I couldn't feel anything but a sense of relief and appreciation for the fact that I was still in one piece. Besides, Perry was pressing Amit for information about the mission—information that the sex-obsessed Indian didn't appear to have.

'I am sorry, Mister Barr, but the Creator told me nothing of a specific nature. All she said was that time is running out, and that I should come and help you in any way I can because the forces of darkness are gathering at an unprecedented rate.'

'She actually said that? Unprecedented? She used that word?'

'Yes,' Amit said.

I dragged myself upright and leaned forward so that the two of them would be able to hear me over the noise of Amit thrashing the engine of the sports car. 'Why?' I asked Perry. 'Is that important?'

He twisted around to look at me and shrugged. 'I'm not sure,' he said, his face heavy with concern. 'She isn't one to exaggerate the achievements of the dark side, and she's seen plenty of them. So if she now says that the forces of darkness are gathering at an unprecedented rate.... Well, it isn't good, let's put it that way.'

Perry turned back and stared at the road ahead. Amit glanced over at him, noticed the growing sense of pessimism in the air, and then grinned broadly.

'Come on, you guys!' His voice was enthusiastic, like that of a televangelist urging his congregation to prove their faith by making a large financial offering. 'We can do this! Doran Salt may be the Ruler of Darkness, the Great Beast, and the most powerful Adversary in the known universe, but look at who he is up against!'

He nodded at me and Perry, and then to himself.

'That isn't a comparison which instills much confidence,' Perry said. 'I mean, think about it. We're just three guys who jumped ship because we couldn't even handle everyday life.'

'No, we are more than that!' Amit said. He paused for a moment as he reached a junction and took a left turn, but quickly continued. 'We are a crack team of divinely appointed commandos who have been given a once-in-an-eternity opportunity to save the world. We are Celestial Stormtroopers. We are Mighty Warriors. We are Heavenly Knights. We are Cosmic Crusaders—'

'And we're almost there.' Perry indicated the building in the distance that looked just as deserted as it had the first time we had seen it.

Amit almost looked disappointed to have had his motivational speech cut short, but nodded his understanding and forced his attention back to the road. He turned off the headlights and slowed the engine to a crawl, presumably to reduce the chances of anyone noticing our arrival, then finally came to a halt outside the derelict building and switched off the engine.

Once again, Perry twisted around in his seat. 'I shouldn't have to remind you that we need to be careful here, so stay close and stay quiet.' He made a point of looking directly at Amit. 'And that means no heroics. Capiche?'

'Very capiche,' Amit said.

The agent nodded. 'Alright. Let's get this done.'

We stepped out of the car (actually, I clambered out, and not in a particularly elegant manner) and headed towards the heavy black door at the end of the hidden alley, just as Perry and I had done several hours earlier. The place had looked completely abandoned the last time we had visited, so I wasn't too concerned about the deathly silence. What I was concerned about was the fact that the silence wasn't immediately banished by the sound of demonic activity and heavy metal music when Perry turned the handle and opened the door.

The place was empty.

When I say empty, I mean it in the most literal sense of the word. Not only were there absolutely no demons, there were no occupants of any kind. Even the fixtures and fittings were absent. There was no bar at the back of the room, no barrel tables and no dancing cages hanging from the iron girders overhead. It was just an empty warehouse, exactly as it had appeared to be on the outside.

'We're too late,' Perry said. The sound of his voice echoing around the room served as a cruel confirmation of his statement. He scanned the place, frowning, then walked over to the door which had previously been behind the bar, and which had earlier led us to the two demons posing as Natalie and Jenny. He disappeared through it and returned a few moments later, shaking his head. 'There's no sign of them. Salt must have moved everybody out while we were busy squeezing lemons.'

Amit raised his eyebrows at that comment, but was sensible enough not to ask for an explanation. Like me, he could see that Perry wasn't in any mood for small talk.

Amit drove us back to our hotel in silence, left the car to be valet-parked and returned with us to the suite that Perry and I had checked into on our arrival in London. It had been less than twenty-four hours since we had last been here, but it seemed like an age ago. Back then, my biggest concern had been whether or not I could pull off a decent enough impression of Cary Grant to dazzle the famous author Natalie Kaylan. The stakes had been high even then, but now that Salt had managed to abduct Natalie and her agent, they seemed even higher... as if I didn't care quite so much about facing the end of the world as I did about having Natalie around to face it with me.

That was an insane perspective, I know. The end of the world would be a global catastrophe—quite literally—but in my mind it didn't matter half as much as not being able to rescue Natalie before the coming apocalypse transpired. Every time I thought of her in Salt's clutches, my stomach lurched, my insides twisted and I felt physically sick. What the hell was all that about?

And then it hit me.

'Oh, shit.'

Perry and Amit were preparing drinks at the bar. Amit was pulling the second of two pints and Perry was pouring himself his customary soda water.

'Problem?' Perry asked as he took himself to the couch and sat down.

'I think I'm in love.'

Amit grinned as he came to hand me one of the pints. 'Congratulations, my friend. That is excellent news!'

'And it's kinda the whole point of us being here, remember?' Perry said.

'Yeah, but still...' I said. 'I mean, I know that we were supposed to be soul mates and stuff, but... the idea of me actually falling in love with her hadn't really occurred to me.'

The agent gave me a sideways glance. The kind of glance that an impatient teacher might give to a particularly slow pupil. 'It's strange to think that one of your direct descendants will be a genius.'

Amit laughed as he joined Perry on the sofa. 'Yes,' he said. 'And it proves that God really does work in mysterious ways.'

'Funny,' I said. 'But I don't see that God is doing much work at all.'

Perry looked puzzled by my comment. 'How do you mean?'

I took a seat opposite them. 'She doesn't seem to be doing anything to help us out, that's all. She has just as much to lose as we do if we fail in this thing, so why can't she intervene?'

'She did intervene,' Perry said. 'That's why Amit's here.'

'Yes, but—and no offense to Amit—she could do a lot more, couldn't she? I mean, if God is present everywhere at the same time, she could tell us where Natalie and Jenny are. If she's all-powerful, she could just beam them out of there, like they do in Star Trek. And if she's all-knowing, she could have given us advance warning about being deceived by demon impostors.'

Perry nodded. 'I used to feel pretty much the same way, when I first started doing this kind of thing. But the truth is, it just doesn't work like that.'

'Why not?'

'Because God isn't some kind of puppet master who goes around pulling strings to make people behave exactly as she wants them to behave. She's more like the inventor of a game. She set up the rules to begin with, but she doesn't dictate who should win or who should lose. She might shout the odd piece of advice in our direction every now and then, but how well or how poorly we play the game is up to us.'

'I like that analogy,' Amit said. 'And if we think about it further, we are all most fortunate, after having played the game so poorly the first time, that the Creator saw fit to give each of us a second chance.'

Perry nodded his agreement, and I quickly realised that I was the odd one out in this scenario. Amit was revelling in the opportunity that he'd been given to test his potential as a special agent, and Perry had been doing it for so many years that he'd simply got used to figuring everything out for himself. It was only me who seemed to expect God to actually act like a god.

'Go get some sleep,' Perry told me. 'You look like you could use it.'

He was right. It was now four in the morning, which was way past my bedtime and not at all the kind of hour in which my brain could realistically be expected to operate in any useful way.

'And what about you two?'

'I'm used to this kind of thing,' Perry said. 'So I'll stay up for a while and try to find a lead on where the girls might be.'

'And if it is acceptable to Mister Barr, I would be most happy to stay awake also,' Amit added. 'To be perfectly honest, I am so excited to be here that I could not possibly sleep even if I tried.'

Perry nodded again and Amit smiled broadly, like a kid who'd just been granted permission to stay up late to watch a horror movie double bill on TV. As for me, I was too knackered to argue, so I set my untouched pint down on the table in front of Amit and shuffled silently off to bed.

CHAPTER TWENTY

When I woke up the next morning, it was with the mistaken belief that I was back home in Brighton, so as I opened my eyes I expected to be greeted by the sight of the large Tennis Girl poster on my bedroom wall. Instead, I found myself gazing at a generic reproduction of an old landscape on canvas, and hearing the muffled sound of Perry and Amit talking in the next room.

I groaned in protest. My old life might have been boring, but this new one was exhausting. Given the option, I would have liked nothing better than to turn back the clock and return to my hitherto banal existence as a humble shelf-stacker.

And then I remembered Natalie.

I'd been able to sleep safe and sound in the comfort of a five-star hotel bedroom, but where had she spent the night? Would Doran Salt have given a damn about her welfare? Or about Jenny's? I doubted it, given that his only concern was to ensure the failure of my mission by keeping me and Natalie apart. I'd been given three days to help her recognise the fact that we were meant to be together, and thereby get things back on track to fulfil some perfectly orchestrated divine plan. But, here I was, on the third day already, and I was no closer to achieving that goal than I had been at the outset. My only hope was that Perry and Amit had been able to find out where Salt might have taken the girls so that we could have one final stab at carrying out another rescue mission. Preferably one that would be a lot more fruitful than the last.

Perry was sitting at the table in the main room. He was staring at the screen of a laptop as he sipped from a cup of coffee which Amit had just poured for him.

'Ah, good morning, my friend,' Amit said when he saw me pad towards them in my hotel robe and complimentary slippers. 'Would you also like a stimulating cup of hot black coffee?'

'Yeah, sure,' I replied. That was about as much enthusiasm as I could ever muster first thing in the morning.

He set about pouring a second cup of coffee whilst Perry remained engrossed at the computer. The senior agent didn't acknowledge my presence until I stood looking over his shoulder.

'Hey,' he said, without looking away from the screen.

'Where did you get the laptop?'

'Hotel concierge.'

Amit brought me my coffee and I nodded my thanks. 'This hotel is completely amazing,' he grinned. 'The concierge brings us almost anything that we care to ask for. Snacks, drinks, laptop computers... I dare say that he would even get us one or two professional lady friends if we were to find ourselves in need of their services.'

'Actually, I'm not sure that the One Who Pays the

Credit Card Bill would be too pleased with us using her money to rent hookers,' Perry said.

Amit's smile faded, but then quickly returned. 'Well, perhaps she will feel differently about that once we have succeeded in our quest. Or perhaps she would even see fit to reward us personally...' He raised one eyebrow at the prospect, then poured himself a coffee and took it over to the sofa.

Perry watched him sit down and then rolled his eyes before returning his attention to the screen. 'Your friend is a frickin' pervert.' He delivered the statement in a tone that was deliberately loud enough for Amit to hear.

'She is a very attractive deity!' Amit called back. 'And if she did not intend for me to revel in the use of my manhood, she would not have bestowed it upon me in the first place.'

It was far too early for me to get involved in that kind of conversation, so I distracted myself by looking down at Perry's laptop screen as I drank my coffee. A Google search page was open and displaying the results for 'London Casinos'.

'Why casinos?'

'Because I've spent all night searching everywhere for a clue as to where the girls might be, and I've drawn a complete blank.'

'Right,' I said, not seeing any connection between the question I had posed and the answer he had given. 'So, why casinos?'

'There was a girl I spent some time with on one of my previous cases. Her name was Lola.'

'Don't tell me, she was a showgirl, right?'

'Right,' he said, completely oblivious to my poor

attempt to be funny. 'She was a cute little thing, and we struck up a really close friendship, but eventually she drifted over to the dark side.'

'Mister Barr is hoping that enough of their friendship may have survived for her to tell him where Doran Salt is gathering his army of darkness.'

'And did you find her?' I asked.

Perry nodded and switched browser tabs to show me a Facebook profile. The name Lola Noir was at the head of the page, and the profile photo showed a good-looking pixie-nosed girl with short black hair that had been partially coloured with streaks of bright crimson. She looked to be in her mid-twenties.

'According to this, she's working as a croupier for a casino in London, so I just need to find out which one so that we can pay her a visit.'

'Sounds like a plan,' I said. 'She's younger than I expected, though.'

'No, she just looks that way. She looked exactly the same the last time I saw her, and that was in the summer of seventy-six.'

The cogs in my brain squeaked as they cranked through what should have been a fairly rudimentary test of mental arithmetic, but it was still early and I was only halfway through my first coffee of the day.

'She's in her sixties, if that's what you're wondering,' Perry said. 'And yes, she probably still looks like that today. It's one of the perks of selling your soul, apparently. The chicks love it.'

I waited for Perry to say that he was joking, but he wasn't smiling, so I looked back at the photo on the screen and allowed myself to indulge in a long moment of barefaced incredulity.

'She is a very hot old lady, isn't she?' Amit said with a chuckle. 'I am very much looking forward to making her acquaintance.'

Perry shook his head. 'You're not her type, believe me.'

Amit shrugged. 'We shall see. And, whatever the case, I will at least be able to spend the rest of my days enjoying the loveliness of her countenance in the privacy of my imagination.'

The agent sighed and looked up at me. 'See what I mean? A frickin' pervert.'

———

By the time I had finished my coffee and taken my morning shower, Perry had identified Lola's place of work as a fairly new casino in the West End. It wasn't one that I'd ever heard of, but that wasn't any great surprise, considering the low-key preferences of Salt's associates and my own general ignorance of most places outside of Brighton. Fortunately, our sports car was equipped with a decent satellite navigation system, and that, along with Amit's rather enthusiastic ignorance of the Highway Code, enabled us to reach the venue at just before midday.

'I'm sorry, but I'm afraid she doesn't start until two,' the casino reception manager told us when we asked about Lola's whereabouts. He was a wiry figure in a house-issue waistcoat, and he sported a gold-coloured name badge which introduced him as Anton. 'Is there anyone else who might be able to help you?'

Perry shook his head. 'It's a personal visit. We're old friends.'

'Ah, I see,' Anton said. 'Well, in that case I can give you some temporary membership cards and you can feel free to wait for her here, if you'd like to.'

The agent nodded and Anton set about writing each of our names onto cards before handing them to us and sending us in the direction of the main gaming area. The casino was one of those 'open 24 hours' venues that presumably made it easy for problem gamblers to stay that way, but apart from a few die-hard members playing slot machines and a couple of businessmen sitting in the bar area, the place was empty. Perry led the way to a blackjack table, where he took a seat and indicated for Amit and myself to do likewise.

Perry reached into the inside pocket of his jacket, felt around for something and then removed a thin wad of bank notes. He peeled off a few and placed them on the table.

'Change, please.'

The dealer at the table—a fairly nondescript guy whose pallid complexion suggested that he didn't get to see very much sunlight—scooped up the notes and set a stack of casino chips in front of Perry.

'Do either of you play?' Perry asked.

Amit shook his head.

'I understand the concept,' I said, 'but I've never played.'

'Well, we have two hours to kill. You might as well learn something while we're waiting.'

And so began an impromptu lesson on how to play blackjack. He started by explaining the aim of the game, which was to get a higher hand than the dealer without going over a total of 21, and went on to take us through the main rules. He demonstrated by playing a few hands, and winning just over half of them, then began delving into what he called Basic Strategy. I tried to keep up with what he was saying about splitting, doubling down and why taking an insurance bet against the dealer having a blackjack was a losing proposition over the long term, but I probably only grasped a small percentage of what he told us. Amit also looked a bit lost, but Perry was so into his own explanations that he didn't seem to notice.

After half an hour, he had approximately doubled his original chip stack, so he divided the winnings between Amit and myself and got us to play alongside him, coaching us on what would be the best decision for every starting hand we were dealt. The rules and strategy points that Perry had explained began to sink in a bit more as I was actually playing, and I was soon rather enjoying myself, probably because I seemed to be winning more often than I lost. Amit was enjoying similar luck, and the stacks of chips in front of us grew steadily as time went on.

We were sipping complimentary soft drinks when Lola arrived to switch places with the dealer. I had suspected that her Facebook profile picture might have been carefully selected to show her in the best possible light, but she was even prettier in the flesh. She also looked even younger, if that were possible, with her short black hair—which was now streaked with bright blue—contrasting nicely with soft fresh skin that put the previous dealer's sallow countenance to shame. A dangling pair of silver butterfly earrings sparkled as she moved.

'Hey, Lola,' Perry said when she had completed the handover and taken up her position behind the blackjack table. 'Long time, no see.'

She automatically looked up from the tray of casino chips that she was checking, and smiled, probably as she did every day of the week to every other customer who said hello. But then she saw the man who had greeted her and her jaw dropped. 'Perry?'

'Well, at least you still remember me.' He smiled at her, but it was the kind of smile that was tinged with some unspoken sadness, like one that a disappointed father might give to his wayward daughter.

Lola frowned, like the very same wayward daughter. 'Of course I remember you.'

'You said you'd keep in touch,' he said. 'Promised, in fact.'

'Yeah. But things changed, you know?'

He nodded. 'You defected.'

'Yeah, I guess.'

They held eye contact for a long moment, then Lola deliberately broke the connection by returning her attention to the chip rack and noting down various totals on her notepad.

'I need a favour,' Perry said.

She responded without looking up. 'What kind of favour?'

'I need you to tell me where you-know-who is gathering his forces.'

Lola looked around nervously, fearing that someone might have overheard. When she was satisfied that nobody had, she simply shook her head. 'You know I can't do that.'

'I know you're not supposed to,' Perry said. 'But we were friends once, and this is really important.'

'You wouldn't betray the woman upstairs for friendship.'

'No. But I'd be willing to bend the rules a little.'

'Even for someone like me?'

'Especially for someone like you.'

She smiled at that. The smile that the wayward daughter might give her overprotective father when she finally realises that he only ever has her best interests at heart. Then, once again, the smile faded and she swallowed hard. 'I'm sorry,' she said. 'I wish I could help you, but I can't.'

Perry exhaled sharply, his lips tight. 'Do you have any idea what's happening right now?'

'No,' she admitted. 'But I assume it's something big or the forces wouldn't be gathering and you wouldn't be coming to me for favours.'

'It's not just big,' he said. 'It's frickin' monstrous. And if I don't find out where the armies are being gathered, it'll soon be game over for everyone.'

She eyed him carefully, then glanced at me and Amit, as if noticing us for the first time. For a moment, I thought that Perry's powers of persuasion were beginning to work, but I was proved wrong when she shook her head and placed both of her hands on the table, just as the previous dealer had done throughout his shift.

'Are you guys here to play blackjack or not?'

I looked at Amit, who looked right back at me, clueless

about what the correct response might be. We both looked at Perry and waited.

'Great idea,' he said. 'What's the table limit?'

'Two grand a hand is the standard. Higher limits by arrangement with the management.'

'So how about we raise the limit and play for it?' he asked.

Lola rolled her eyes.

'No, hear me out,' he said. 'I'll take one thousand pounds in chips, and if I can turn it into five thousand in the next thirty minutes, all you have to do is point us in the right direction. Just name a place and help narrow things down for us.'

Her eyes narrowed as she considered his proposition. 'Turn five hundred into fifty thousand and you've got yourself a deal,' she said. 'But if you win, I get to keep the winnings too, and if you lose, you have to go home and quit bugging me.'

She was a tough negotiator, I'll give her that, but her terms were ridiculous. A winning hand in this game only paid even money, so a bet of twenty pounds would get us forty pounds back, effectively doubling our stake. The best possible winning hand, a blackjack, would pay us slightly better odds of three to two, giving us fifty pounds back from a bet of twenty, but even that was only achievable by getting a total of twenty-one with the first two cards dealt. Add in the fact that Perry had once committed suicide because he'd been unable to succeed in gambling, and the idea of us being able to turn five hundred pounds into fifty thousand in half an hour was just crazy.

'Okay,' Perry said. 'It's a deal.'

CHAPTER TWENTY-ONE

'Could you excuse us for a second, please?'

I got up from my seat and stepped away from the blackjack table, motioning for Perry to do the same. The agent looked puzzled, but asked Amit to stay put and keep an eye on our chips before joining me.

'What's up?'

'You're thinking like a crazy person, that's what's up,' I said. 'We don't have a cat in hell's chance of winning that bet, and we really can't afford to waste another half an hour trying.' I held up my wrist and tapped the face of my watch to drive the point home.

'So what do you suggest?' he asked. 'We have no idea where the girls are, and Lola's the only person I know who might be able to point us in the right direction. As for the bet, we just need to play aggressively and hope that we enjoy some good luck.'

'That's the plan? We keep our fingers crossed and hope for the best?'

Perry took a slow, deep breath, the way he always did

when someone was testing his patience. 'Look, in half an hour we'll either have some information that we can use or we'll be a few hundred bucks and thirty minutes down. If you have a better idea then say so now, otherwise we're just wasting even more time discussing this.'

Bastard.

There are three things that I really hate in life. One is militant feminism, which is often just as blatantly sexist as the chauvinistic patriarchy that it claims to oppose. Another is finishing a really good cup of freshly ground coffee with an accidental mouthful of dregs. And the third —which is the one that I was most aware of at that particular moment—is realising halfway through making a seemingly well reasoned argument that my logic is fundamentally flawed.

I could have nodded and said that Perry had a very good point, or I could have apologised for questioning his approach, but since both of those options would have involved admitting that I was wrong, I took neither one of them. Instead, I simply returned to my seat at the table, waited for Perry to follow suit, and made a silent vow to abstain from any and all forms of criticism for the next half hour. The chances were high that I would have the opportunity to say 'I told you so' in the very near future, but if there was even the slimmest hope that the white-haired American could pull off the unlikely gamble and get the information we needed to find Natalie and Jenny, I wasn't going to knowingly jeopardise it.

Lola was impatient to begin the game, presumably because she just wanted to get it over and done with. Perry gathered the chips that Amit and I had been using to play with, added them to his own stack and totalled them up.

'I have three hundred pounds,' he told her. 'So I'll need two hundred more.'

He exchanged another thin wad of notes for the additional chips, then ordered a round of soft drinks whilst waiting for Lola to get approval for raising the game stakes. When she announced that it was done, he flexed his neck from side to side, cracked his knuckles and placed the palms of his hands on the table.

'Okay, Lola,' he said. 'Let's do this.'

Although the rest of the casino was still rather empty, the atmosphere around our blackjack table was thick with a heady mix of tension, fear and excitement. Lola quickly slipped into stony-faced dealer mode and eyed Perry like a hawk as he placed a bet of one hundred pounds on the table and nodded for her to begin. The first card that he was dealt was a ten of clubs. The second was a nine of hearts, giving him a hand total of nineteen. The dealer's up-card was an ace of clubs.

'Would you like insurance?' Lola asked, her voice devoid of emotion.

Perry shook his head.

She turned over her hole card to reveal a seven of diamonds.

'Dealer plays eighteen,' she said. 'Player has nineteen. Player wins.'

She placed his profit, which amounted to one hundred pounds in chips, in front of him before gathering the cards. Perry left the winnings there, as well as the original bet, for the next hand. He was dealt a king and jack, and his twenty beat Lola's seventeen, giving him another two hundred pounds. He let all four hundred ride on the third bet and scored a winning blackjack, receiving another six hundred in chips and taking his original stake of one hundred pounds to one thousand in less than two minutes.

'I am most impressed, Mister Barr,' Amit said.

Perry grinned. 'Guess it must be my lucky day.'

'Or somebody up there likes you,' Amit said, pointing to the heavens.

'Don't count your chickens, boys,' Lola warned. 'You're still forty-nine grand away from winning the bet, and lucky streaks don't last forever.'

Perry looked at Lola for a moment and sniffed, then nodded in agreement. 'She's right,' he said. 'We need to speed things up a little.'

He clawed his stack of chips towards him and placed a new, lower bet of one hundred pounds in the box directly in front of him. He then placed the same stake in the boxes to his immediate left and right so that he could play three hands at once. 'Bring it on, Lola.'

For the next fifteen minutes, Perry Barr played black-jack like a pro. I don't know if it was due to skill, divine providence or blind luck, but by playing three hands simultaneously he somehow managed to make a profit or break even every time. He also seemed to know exactly when to let his bets ride and when to reduce the stakes, as if he had some kind of sixth sense that helped him to maximise the winning streaks and minimise the impact of hands that weren't so good. I'd seen poker players demon-strate similar intuitive abilities on late-night television shows, but to actually sit next to someone who seemed to be able to predict what would happen in the next few moments, not just once, but over and over again, and amass a pile of money as a result, was pretty incredible.

By the time he was halfway through the allotted thirty minutes, Perry had progressed to playing five hands at a time, and had turned his initial chip stack of five hundred pounds into a much larger one worth thirty thousand. I know it was that much because he had been keeping a tally on his performance and had been announcing his balance at regular intervals throughout the game. Quite how he was managing to keep track of so many hands without suffering any decline in performance was beyond me, but he seemed to know exactly what he was doing, and was capitalising on his intuitive knack for staking far more money on the winning hands than he was risking on the losing hands. At this point, if someone had told me that Perry Barr was a genuine psychic, I would have been sorely tempted to believe them.

Perry continued demonstrating his considerable blackjack skills, and five minutes later he had a total of forty thousand pounds in front of him. With another ten minutes to go, I allowed myself to relax, but not completely. There now seemed little doubt that Perry would win the bet, but I was beginning to wonder whether Lola would be willing to keep her side of the bargain when he did. Whilst Perry had described her as an old friend, her defection to the dark side had naturally shifted her loyalties, and there was really no reason to believe that she would willingly betray Doran Salt just because she had lost a side bet at the blackjack table. So, what would happen then?

'Right,' Perry said. 'Let's finish this thing quickly, shall we?'

He stacked all of his chips neatly in front of him, in four columns, allowing himself a moment to perform an impromptu trick which involved rolling the very last chip from one side of his hand to the other before placing it on top of the fourth column. Then, with the kind of confident flourish that I'd seen Texas Hold'em players display at the final table of the World Series of Poker, he shoved an entire column of chips into the betting box directly in front of him.

'Deal,' he said.

Lola looked at the stack of chips, and then up at Perry. 'You want to bet ten grand on a single hand?'

'Is that a problem?'

The dealer shook her head, and the silver butterflies that dangled from her ears swayed from side to side as she did so. 'No,' she said. 'I was just checking, that's all.'

Perry nodded.

Lola dealt the cards. Perry received a king and a nine. The dealer's up card was a jack, so Perry chose to stand. Lola checked her other card and flipped over an ace.

'Dealer has blackjack. Player has nineteen. Dealer wins.'

She scraped the column of chips towards her and placed them neatly in the rack on her side of the table.

Perry look at the cards, stunned.

'Did we just lose ten grand?' I asked. My question wasn't directed at anyone in particular, but was purely for the benefit of my own ears, because my brain was clearly having some difficulty accepting the fact that such a thing was possible in such a short period of time. The hand had taken about ten seconds to deal, and another ten to play out, which meant that we'd just lost around five hundred pounds per second.

'You win some, you lose some,' Lola said with a smirk.

'It was just a blip,' Perry said. He riffled his chips and shoved another column into the box. 'Let's try again, shall we?'

I watched as Lola dealt another hand. Perry was dealt a queen and an eight, giving him eighteen. Lola's up-card was an ace.

'Would you like insurance?'

Perry shook his head. The dealer checked her hole card, then flipped it over to reveal a queen.

'Dealer has blackjack,' she said. 'Player has eighteen. Dealer wins.'

'Goddamn it,' Perry snarled. 'How many aces do you have in there?' He stood up and walked a few paces away from the table, then looked back at Lola as she raked in our second bet of ten thousand pounds and gathered up the cards. Perry's face was red, not with embarrassment, but with anger. He looked at me and Amit, then tightened his lips and returned to his seat.

'I'm going all-in,' he said to nobody in particular.

'Are you mad?' I asked. I know that it wasn't the most sensible thing to ask a guy who had just dropped twenty grand on two hands of cards, but going all-in meant risking everything that we had left in the middle of what looked very much like the beginning of a losing streak.

Perry checked his watch and looked at me. 'We have less than eight minutes left to make another thirty grand,' he said. 'If we don't double-up now we won't have a chance anyway.'

We wouldn't have needed to double-up if he hadn't

played the last two hands like some kind of compulsive gambling freak, but I didn't see how pointing out that fact would have helped the situation, so I tried a different approach.

'Couldn't we at least pull the stakes back a little?' I asked. 'If we dropped back to a couple of thousand per hand we'd still have a shot at making the fifty thousand target, and if necessary we could go all-in when we only have a minute or two left. Best of both worlds.'

'We only need two winning hands to succeed if we do things my way,' he said.

'Only one if we are fortunate enough to get a black-jack,' Amit added.

I scowled my disapproval at my former cellmate, but he failed to notice.

'Exactly,' Perry said. 'We've had two losing hands in a row, so we're due some luck, right?' He pushed the two remaining columns of chips into the betting box. 'Twenty thousand on the next hand.'

'I am wishing you the very best of British,' Amit told him.

Perry allowed a smile. 'Thanks, pal. It's nice to have a fellow optimist around at times like this.' He shot me an accusing look, then returned his attention to the table. 'Come on, Lola. Be good to me.'

She eyed the chips carefully and dealt the cards for the next hand. Perry received a king of hearts and a nine of clubs. The dealer's up-card was an eight of diamonds. Lola wasn't happy. She flipped over her hole card to reveal a nine of diamonds, for a hand of seventeen.

'Dealer has seventeen. Player has nineteen. Player wins.'

'Yes!' Amit whooped with a grin. 'We have the winning hand. May all praise be to her divinely plump gorgeousness.'

Whilst I thought that Amit's evangelical outburst was a tad embarrassing, I couldn't help but feel equally thrilled with the result. In a single hand, Perry had brought us back to where we had been before the commencement of his recklessness, which was just ten thousand pounds short of the fifty thousand goal.

I checked the time. 'We still have six minutes. Let's be careful now, shall we?'

Perry added the winnings to his pile before looking at me, and then at Amit.

'How about we drop back to five grand?' he asked. 'Means we need to win two more hands than the house does in the next few minutes.'

'Sounds reasonable,' I said.

Amit nodded his eager agreement.

Perry split the chips into eight smaller columns of five thousand each and slid one of them across the baize into the betting box for the next hand.

Which promptly lost.

He bet another column on a second hand.

Which also lost.

Perry shook his head and sighed. At this point, I feared that he would go mad again and risk more, but he surprised me and—quite sensibly, I thought—bet another five thousand on the third hand.

Lola didn't even attempt to conceal her smile when she won that one too.

We now had three minutes left, and we were right back down to twenty-five thousand pounds.

'We really need to double-up now,' Perry said.

He waited for nods of agreement from Amit and myself, then slid the five remaining columns of chips into the betting box.

Amit closed his eyes, clasped his hands together and started praying silently.

Lola dealt us a pair of tens. Her up-card was a six.

Perry smiled. 'We'll stand,' he said.

Lola flipped the hole card to reveal a five.

The smile on Perry's face faded.

She took a third card from the shoe and flipped it over to reveal a jack.

'Dealer has twenty-one. Player has twenty. Dealer wins.'

And with that, our ambitious bet to try and win information leading to the whereabouts of Natalie and Jenny went completely down the pan.

Perry sat staring at the cards on the table for several long moments, then dejectedly looked up at the dealer. 'Lola, please. I need your help.'

'I know,' she said. 'And I gave you a chance, but you lost the bet.'

The agent continued looking at her, probably hoping to see a glimmer of sympathy, empathy or even pity in her eyes, but there was none of that. Her stare was cold and empty of anything but a faint whiff of contempt.

Perry nodded, then slowly rose from his seat, his head bowed. Amit and I watched in silence as he turned away from the table and shuffled wearily towards the bar on the other side of the casino floor.

CHAPTER TWENTY-TWO

Perry was already ordering his second shot of bourbon by the time we reached him. Had he not sworn off the stuff decades earlier, it wouldn't have been a big deal, but seeing him fall off the wagon after more than half a century was another matter entirely. He was sitting on a tall stool, his elbows resting on the bar in front of him, and he was frowning at his reflection in the mirror on the wall opposite. He didn't seem to notice when Amit and I sat down on either side of him.

'We shouldn't be surprised,' I told him. 'The house always wins in the end. That's why these places exist.'

'I don't mind them winning in the end,' he said. 'Just not today.'

'You did your best.'

'No,' he said. 'I messed up. Again. Just like I always did. Same old story.'

He downed the bourbon in one, bared his teeth and nodded for the barman to pour him another.

'Drinking won't help,' I said. 'You know that.'

'It'll help me.'

'We need to find the girls.'

He gave me a sideways glance, then shook his head. 'We're more than halfway through the third day. It's too late.'

'Maybe, but we have to try.'

'And how do you propose we do that?' he asked.

It was a question that I didn't have any kind of answer to. I looked over at Amit.

'Perhaps the Creator can assist us once more,' he suggested.

Perry shook his head. 'We were one hand away from winning that bet,' he said. 'If she'd wanted to help us then we wouldn't be sitting here right now, would we?'

Amit frowned. Perry downed his third bourbon in as many minutes and nodded for a fourth. 'Keep 'em coming,' he told the barman.

I stepped away from the bar and motioned for Amit to join me, then spoke quietly to avoid being overheard by the senior agent. 'He'll be next to useless if we don't get him away from here soon.'

'I am very much inclined to agree with you, my friend,' Amit replied. 'But I suspect that Mister Barr is already incapable of listening to reason, and his mood does not appear to be one that we will be able to change easily.'

He was right. Perry was already hitting the bottle hard, and if he was going to listen to reason he would have done so by now.

'Perhaps if you were to petition the Creator yourself...'

'I wouldn't know how,' I said. 'Besides, I don't really see why it would make any difference coming from me.'

'Of course it could make a difference,' Amit said. 'After

all, this is your noble quest, not ours. Mister Barr and I are here merely to assist you.'

He hadn't meant it to do so, but his comment stung, and that was because he'd hit the nail right on the head. This wasn't their quest. They hadn't been the one who had jumped from Brighton Pier for no better reason than boredom, and they weren't the one who had inadvertently started the countdown to the end of the world.

All of this was my doing. I was the one who had created the whole situation, and I was the one who'd been sent to set things right again. The woman upstairs had given me seventy-two hours to sort things out, but more than two-thirds of that time had already been spent, and I'd actually done very little towards achieving the goal. I mean, yes, I'd followed Perry's guidance, but I'd done so reluctantly, and I'd really been relying on the agent to sort things out on my behalf. Even now, I was more concerned with talking him into getting off his arse than I was in trying to figure out some kind of solution for myself.

And then the realisation hit me. This is what I always did. This is how I'd lived my entire life. Always looking for an easy way out. Always avoiding responsibility whenever possible. And always expecting someone else to handle things simply because I couldn't be bothered.

It was bad enough that I'd pretty much wasted my own life by living that way, but now everyone else was beginning to pay the price as well. Natalie and Jenny were God knows where with the Prince of Fucking Darkness, mankind was just hours away from total and utter annihilation, and Perry and Amit were lumbered with someone —namely me—who was doing Jack Shit to put things right.

'You watch Perry for a minute, I need to go and do something,' I said. 'And try to make sure that he doesn't drink much more. Get the barman to water the stuff down if you need to.'

Amit raised his eyebrows at my request, probably because he was as surprised as I was by my sudden change in attitude, but he didn't argue. 'Of course, my friend,' he said. 'We will wait here until you return.'

As I turned to walk back towards Lola's blackjack table on the other side of the casino floor, I noticed that I felt quite different to the way I had felt when heading towards the bar just a few minutes earlier. In fact, I felt something that I had never felt before. I don't know what it was, but it was something good. I was standing taller, there was a sense of purpose in my stride that even Cary Grant would have been proud of, and for the first time in my life I just knew that I was going to take my fate in my own hands and start sorting things out for myself.

Lola was dealing for an overweight guy in a business suit when I arrived back at the blackjack table. She eyed me carefully, but said nothing. I waited for their hand to play out and then tapped the man on the shoulder.

'This table is closing now,' I said. 'There's another one over there if you'd like to continue playing.' I pointed to a table in the distance, where a blonde girl was dealing for a man who seemed to be more interested in the shape of her breasts than in the cards being dealt in front of him.

The businessman looked up at me and was about to protest, but I stared him down and he begrudgingly gathered his chips and shuffled off without saying a word. I took his seat as soon as he'd vacated it.

'He thought you were his friend,' I said.

Lola was stony-faced. 'Well, he thought wrong.'

'No, he didn't. You're still his friend. Or, at least, you'd like to be. You're just too chickenshit to stand up to Doran Salt, that's all.'

She smiled awkwardly. It was a nervous smile. One that told me I'd touched a nerve.

'Have you really thought things through?'

'What do you mean?'

'Well, I assume that you know what's happening,' I said. 'Why he's gathering his forces, I mean.'

She shrugged casually. 'There are gatherings every few years. There always have been.'

'This one is different.'

'Oh yeah? Why?'

'Because this time he's preparing for the end of the world.'

Lola giggled at the statement, then saw that I was glaring at her, and the smile disappeared from her face.

'You're serious?'

'I wish I weren't,' I said. 'Mostly because I'm the one who's responsible for the whole thing.'

'How come?'

'I don't have time to go into that right now,' I said. 'All I can tell you is that I've got until midnight tonight to prevent it from happening, and to do that, I need to know where Salt is.'

She shook her head. 'I'm sorry, I can't. Betraying Doran would get me killed.'

'So I was right. You're scared.'

There was a long pause as she considered the observation, then she nodded a nervous admission. 'Wouldn't you be?' she asked.

'Of course I would,' I said. 'Hell, I'm scared shitless right now. But I've come to realise that being scared isn't a good enough excuse to avoid doing the right thing, especially when other people are relying on you to help them out.'

She nodded briefly, almost imperceptibly, and at that moment I knew that she was listening—really listening—to what I was saying. That meant there was a chance that my words were convincing her, but if I said the wrong thing, or I presented my case in the wrong way, I might blow it, so I paused to process my thoughts carefully before continuing.

'Do you really think you'll be any safer when there's nobody else around to prevent Salt from doing whatever he wants?'

Lola said nothing. Maybe I needed to take a different approach.

'Look,' I said. 'Whatever team you're on... deep down, you're a good person. Perry wouldn't call you his friend if that weren't the case.'

She looked across the casino floor, to where Perry was slumped over the bar, and frowned.

'It's never too late to turn things around,' I said. 'And if you're worried about betraying Salt, you don't even have to tell me outright where he is. Just give me enough of a clue to put us on the right track. That way you can help us and protect yourself at the same time.'

'And what makes you think you'll be able to stop whatever it is that's going down?' she asked. 'You say you're trying to prevent the end of the world, but how will you be able to do that?'

'I honestly don't know that I will,' I said. 'All I know is

that I'll give it my best shot. But I won't have any chance at all if I don't even know where the bad guy is.'

An oversized pit boss with a bald head and a goatee beard approached the table. 'Everything okay here, Lola?' He was looking me up and down carefully, but I pretended not to notice.

'Yes,' she said. 'It's okay, he's a friend. But thanks.'

'Any time,' he nodded, and he went on his way just as quickly as he had appeared on the scene.

Lola waited for him to get some distance away before turning back to me. She eyed me for a long moment, then reached under the table and produced a napkin and a pen. She wrote something quickly on the napkin, and then folded it and put it in my hand. 'That's all I can give you, but if you're serious it should be more than enough. Ask Perry to check back with me when you've done whatever needs to be done, yeah? I have a few decisions that I might like to unmake.'

I took the napkin and put it straight in my pocket. 'I will, I promise,' I said. 'And thank you. Hang tight and if it all goes well he'll get back to you before you know it.'

She allowed herself to smile at the thought and nodded, then I left the table and headed back to the bar to tell Perry and Amit the good news. As I walked, I took the napkin from my pocket and unfolded it. She had written just a single word on it, in large capital letters:

DONINGTON

CHAPTER TWENTY-THREE

Twenty minutes later, we were back in the convertible—with the roof now in place—and Amit was getting annoyed by his inability to drive us out of London at his usual demented pace. Traffic was heavy, tourists were happily risking their lives by squeezing through any and every gap that appeared between the slow-moving cars, and London cab drivers were routinely demonstrating their ownership of the roads by cutting us up at every opportunity.

'What is wrong with the people who live in this city?' he asked. 'They are so shockingly rude it is driving me insane.'

'I blame sex, drugs and rock n roll,' Perry said. 'Good manners went out of style when the Beatles came in.'

'Wasn't rock n roll a fifties thing?' I asked.

'Yes, I am almost certain that you are right,' Amit agreed. 'And if I am not very much mistaken, sex and drugs also existed long before then.'

I smirked at Amit's comment, but Perry didn't seem to

be too impressed by it. 'Just because something existed back then doesn't mean that we fixated on it like a pack of animals,' he said. 'How long will it take us to get to this place once we're out of the city?'

Amit looked at the sat nav screen on the dashboard. 'About two hours from the motorway, but how long it will take us to get to that point given the current flow of traffic, I have no idea.'

Perry nodded, then leaned his head back on the rest and closed his eyes. 'Wake me up when we're thirty minutes away,' he said. 'I have some bourbon to sleep off.'

We were heading towards Donington Park in the East Midlands, but at this point we weren't exactly sure why. We'd looked the place up on Google (what people used to do before smartphones is beyond me) and noted that it was most famous for its motor racing track. One site fairly close to that track was also used to host the annual Download rock music festival. That event had concluded several weeks earlier, but the same venue was now hosting a brand new 'darker metal' festival called Ambusti Terrae, which Google helpfully translated as 'scorched earth'. Perry had suggested that this would be a perfect location for Salt to gather his army, because the locals were already used to seeing thousands of heavy metal fans in the area, and so a similarly sized crowd of Salt's minions would be unlikely to raise any eyebrows.

Quite how we would be able to tell if Salt was using Ambusti Terrae as some kind of cover, I had no idea. We also had no idea if Salt had in fact taken Natalie and Jenny with him to Donington Park or whether he had holed them up elsewhere. If it was the former, we still had a chance, however slight or unlikely, of getting to them and making them safe, but if it was the latter... well, we'd basically be screwed.

'Perhaps you should try and get some rest too, my friend,' Amit said. He was looking at me through the rearview mirror. 'The coming hours may be very taxing for you.'

'Yeah, maybe you're right,' I said. 'But give me a shout if you need anything, won't you?'

'Most definitely. And may you have the most pleasant of dreams in the meantime.'

'Thanks,' I said. 'I'll do my best.'

I twisted myself around sideways and made the great effort that was required to recline on the back seat. It was only about half as long as I needed, but by curling my knees up to my chest like an overgrown foetus, I somehow managed to get into a position that was only marginally uncomfortable. I closed my eyes, not really expecting to be able to sleep with the sound of the traffic and the seemingly endless problems that were assaulting us lately, but I think my body still hadn't adequately recovered from the ordeal of the last few days, because I soon found myself drifting off.

'Time is running out, Mr Fenton.'

Startled, I opened my eyes, but instead of being on the back seat of the car, which was where I'd left my body just a moment earlier, I found myself standing on an expansive and impossibly fluffy white cloud that was floating in the middle of a bright blue sky. About ten feet in front of me was a large silver throne, upon which sat the owner of the voice that had addressed me by name.

It was Her, the Creator of the Universe, in all of her intimidating glory. She was wearing a flowing white gown, a silver crown and large silver lightning bolts that hung from her earlobes.

'Don't just stand there,' she growled. 'Say something.'

I'd met some scary women in my time, but this one was something else entirely. Like a FEMEN protestor armed with a sparkly pink hand grenade and a bad case of PMS.

'Yes,' I said, or rather stammered. 'I know. And I'm really sorry that it's taken me so long, but I'm on the case now. We're on our way to Donington Park.'

'I'm well aware of where you're going,' she said. 'What I want to know is what you expect to do when you get there.'

'Well,' I said, stalling for time as I began scrambling around for ideas—any ideas at all—about how to answer. 'The first thing will be to find out where the girls are.'

'And then?'

'And then we'll rescue them.'

'And then you'll rescue them,' she repeated. 'Just like that.' Her tone was condescending, and probably rightfully so.

'Well, it won't be easy...'

'You don't say.' Her nostrils flared and the lightning bolts which dangled from her ears crackled with electricity.

'No,' I said. 'I know what's at risk, I really do. And I promise you that I'll do everything I can to make things right.'

She stared at me for a long moment, and then sniffed dismissively.

'Look, I want this to work out as much as you do,' I told her.

'Because you're scared of what will happen if you don't?'

'No. Maybe in the beginning, yes. But now it's not about me. It's about everyone else. Perry and Amit, obviously, and Jenny too, but to be honest it's mostly about Natalie. She's the most amazing woman I've ever met. I don't know what I did to deserve her.'

'You did absolutely nothing to deserve her,' God said. 'As I told you previously, all you did was get disgustingly lucky in a cosmic lottery. And then you went and threw away the ticket.'

I nodded. 'Yes. And I know that it was stupid of me to do that, so now I'm going to pick it back up.'

She stared at me, long and hard. 'Do not fail me, Mr Fenton, or I will soon be removing your testicles and hanging them from your nipples.' She paused and grinned cruelly. 'With corroded fishing hooks.'

I awoke with a start, and instinctively reached down to check that my balls were still where I had last left them.

They were.

Relieved, I sat upright and saw that we were just pulling off the motorway. Perry was already awake and gave me a nod.

'Good timing,' he said. 'We're almost there.'

'Already?'

'You have been sleeping for more than two hours,' Amit said. 'So I trust that you are now feeling fully refreshed and ready for the most heinous battle that lies ahead.'

'As ready as I'll ever be,' I said.

Amit gave me a wide-eyed look through the rear-view mirror. 'I must commend you on your stiff upper lip,' he said. 'If I were in your shoes, I would be wanting to throw myself off Brighton Pier all over again.'

Perry looked at him and frowned, but Amit didn't notice.

'Why?' I asked, although I knew that it was probably a mistake to do so even before the word had vacated my mouth.

'Because you will soon be sparring one-on-one with the most formidable enemy in the known universe,' he said matter-of-factly. 'The Infernal One is no amateur when it comes to disemboweling his foes. In fact, he is said to make it look ridiculously easy.'

Amit smiled a satisfied smile, as if he had just given me the most useful piece of information that ever existed. I did my best to return the expression, but it probably just looked like I had a bad case of wind.

'Has anyone ever told you that you'd make a great motivational speaker?' Perry asked.

Amit looked puzzled. 'No, not that I recall.'

'Well, that's because you'd suck at it, big time. So it's probably best that you just stick to driving, yeah?'

Amit considered the agent's rhetorical question, then shrugged and nodded. 'Of course, you are right, Mister Barr. I am here to serve the mission in whatever way you see fit, and if it is to be confined to driving then I will continue to drive to the very best of my ability for as long as is necessary.'

Perry rolled his eyes at the verbose response, then turned around in his seat to face me. 'Forget the disemboweling stuff,' he said. 'You know the rules. Salt can't lay a finger on you. And if he breaks the rules, he loses the right to take over if we don't succeed.'

'Yeah, I know,' I said. 'But I'm not worried about me, I'm worried about the girls. There's nothing in the rules about him not being able to harm them.'

'No, but that's implied. Besides, all he really needs to do is keep you and Natalie apart long enough for you to miss the deadline. If he succeeds in doing that, he wins. But if you get to her first, and you get that kiss...'

He let the rest of the sentence complete itself, and I nodded my understanding. The task ahead hadn't been made any easier because of what he'd said, but at least it wasn't quite as daunting as the picture of intestinal spillage that Amit had so kindly painted for me.

We arrived at our intended destination a few minutes later. Actually, I use the word 'arrived' in its loosest possible sense, because the gridlock of the lengthy queue to the parking area made the crawl of central London traffic look dangerously fast by comparison. We had to sit in the queue for half an hour, edging forward inches at a time as we gradually made our way to the people in yellow jackets who were protecting the entrance.

I'd never been to a music festival before, let alone one that specifically catered to heavy metal fans, and the spectacle of hundreds of people milling around, looking like extras from a Cradle of Filth video, was quite something. Many were wearing regular, albeit grubby-looking T-shirts and jeans, but every once in a while we caught sight of someone who had turned things up to eleven by donning as much cow skin and corpse paint as their bodies could carry.

'Don't they know that they stand out like sore thumbs?' I asked, indicating a tall bloke who had painted himself to look like a rotting corpse. 'You'd think they'd take more care to blend in.'

'They aren't Salt's guys,' Perry said. 'They're just pretenders who want to look mean and intimidating as a fashion statement. The real bad guys are usually the ones you'd never suspect in a million years. Like her, for example.'

He was pointing at a sweet-looking woman in her mid-thirties who was wearing the uniform of a St. John's Ambulance volunteer. She was smiling at everyone as she milled around looking for the next golden opportunity to apply a bandage from the bulging first aid kit which hung from her shoulder.

'Are you kidding?'

'Nope.'

'But how can you tell?'

'They have a certain aura. It's a kind of energy field that everyone has, but theirs is different.'

'Different how?'

'It's black,' he said. 'Blacker than you'd ever think possible.'

The woman didn't appear to exude anything other than a desperate desire to show off her resuscitation skills, but then I wasn't the expert on demon spotting. And if I had been—

My train of thought slammed me straight into yet another question.

'Hang on a second. If you can tell which ones are demons and which ones aren't...'

'Then why didn't I realise that the two girls we rescued

from Hell were actually demons all along?'

Exactly.

'Something like that,' I said, being careful to avoid sounding as if I was blaming him for the oversight. I knew that Perry was doing his best—he had been working harder than anyone else to make the mission a success—but if he could tell the difference between the bad guys and the good guys just by looking at their aura, why hadn't he noticed the auras of the demons who had impersonated Natalie and Jenny right at the outset?

'I've been asking myself the same question,' he said.

'And?'

'And I really don't know the answer.' He shrugged. 'Looks like my knowledge of Doran Salt's dark arts isn't quite as comprehensive as I thought.'

His direct and honest admission of fallibility was admirable, but at the same time it was also more than a little disconcerting. Here I was, potentially only hours away from what Amit had rather unhelpfully described as a heinous battle with the most formidable enemy in the known universe, and Perry was now telling me that he didn't have all the answers. I must have known that on some level, because nobody is perfect, but hearing it from the man himself wasn't encouraging.

Perry stared at the St. John's Ambulance demon for a few seconds longer, then pulled his eyes away when one of the yellow jackets who were guarding the car park entrance tapped on the window and indicated for him to roll it down, which he promptly did.

'Tickets please,' said the short bloke in thick brown-framed spectacles.

'We thought we'd be able to buy them here,' Perry told him.

The man shook his head. 'Nah, mate, you can't do that. You need to have got them already.'

Perry reached into his pocket and removed a wad of bank notes. 'Look. I won't even count it, but this is yours if you let us in.'

The guard looked at the notes for a long time, then sniffed and shook his head once again. 'Sorry, mate,' he said. 'I mean, it's bloody tempting, but I'd be risking me job, and I have a wife and kids to think about...'

Perry nodded and smiled, then peeled off five twenties and crammed them into the hand of the attendant. 'Well, take that for you trouble anyway, and treat the family.'

'You're joking,' the man said, clearly surprised by the gesture.

'Nope,' Perry said. 'But if you could tell us where we might be able to buy tickets, I'd really appreciate it.'

The man winced and sucked in a mouthful of air through gritted teeth. 'You'll be lucky, to be honest. But try calling Ticketmaster. They'll tell you if there are any left.'

Perry nodded. 'Thanks. We'll do that.'

Amit waited for Perry's go-ahead to proceed, then pulled away from the car park entrance—leaving behind a rather chuffed attendant—and began following the signs marked EXIT.

'Where do you wish me to drive now, Mister Barr?'

Perry shrugged, sighed thoughtfully and then shrugged again. 'Let's go find some place to sit down and grab a bite to eat,' he said. 'It looks like we need a new plan.'

CHAPTER TWENTY-FOUR

We found a Little Chef diner about five minutes away from the festival site, ordered some food (steak and eggs for Perry, cod and chips for myself, and a vegetable cottage pie for Amit, who turned out to be a strict vegetarian) and then I called Ticketmaster to try and buy our tickets. An apologetic woman on the other end of the line told me that they had completely sold out within hours of them first being made available. Frustrated, I thanked her anyway, ended the call and set my phone down on the table.

'No chance,' I said. 'We'll just have to get in the hard way.'

'Does that mean illegally?' Amit asked, his voice sounding almost excited by the prospect. 'Without tickets?'

I nodded and Amit grinned broadly.

'That might be easier said than done,' Perry said. 'Security in those places tends to be pretty tight.'

'Nothing worth doing is ever easy,' I said.

The agent gave me a sideways glance. 'I'm sorry. Aren't you Gary Fenton?'

'So?'

'So, shouldn't you be quitting at the first hurdle?' He laughed at his jibe, and Amit quickly joined in.

'You're funny,' I said. 'When we're done with this whole saving-the-world thing you should consider a career in stand-up.'

'Okay then, hotshot. Let's hear it. What's your plan?'

My ideas were rather vague and fuzzy to begin with, but over the course of our lunch I outlined a variety of possibilities that I thought had merit and listened to the feedback given by my two heavenly helpers. Together, the three of us tweaked the proposals according to what we all felt made the most sense, and by the time we were finishing our post-lunch mugs of coffee, we had developed a potentially doable plan of action.

'This promises to be quite thrilling,' Amit grinned when I had recapped the approach that we had agreed to take. 'I feel as if I will now be setting aside my James Bond persona and becoming more like Ethan Hunt in Mission Impossible.'

I was very tempted to make a joke about Ethan Hunt and cockney rhyming slang at that point, but Perry must have guessed as much, because he shot me a look of warning and shook his head. Reluctantly, I kept the crude one-liner to myself and allowed Amit to revel in his enthusiasm for his new-found identity.

We returned to the festival site around five hours later,

but this time Amit was wearing dark blue overalls instead of his white suit, and he was driving a similarly coloured pick-up truck instead of the sports car. I was sitting in the passenger seat, also wearing dark blue overalls, and we were both wearing matching blue baseball caps. As for Perry, well... you'll find out soon enough.

This time, we didn't aim for the car park, but for the maintenance entrance, where another guy in a yellow jacket was waiting to check vehicles in and out. This guy was taller than the guard that Perry had tried to bribe several hours earlier, and he had long, greasy hair, as well as a dangerous-looking scar that ran down his left cheek. How he'd acquired the scar was anyone's guess, but he didn't strike me as being the kind of bloke you'd like to run into on a dark and lonely night.

Amit rolled down his window as we approached.

'Evenin,' the man said in a surprisingly friendly tone. 'What can I do you for?'

'We've brought a new crapper for the punters,' Amit said, in what I can only describe as an Oscar-winning Black Country accent. 'To replace the one that's out of commission.'

'Can I have a gander at the paperwork?' the man asked.

'Course you can.' Amit leaned over to grab a sheet of paper from the dashboard and quietly grinned at me as he did so. He'd been the one to suggest preparing a fake delivery document, just in case, and we'd been able to knock one up on a computer in the local library. 'Here you go.'

The attendant took the paperwork and barely gave it a second glance before handing it straight back. 'Okay, mate. Do you want a hand unloading it?'

'Up to you, squire. The old one's full of shit and puke, though, so you'd need to watch out for splashback.'

The guard grimaced at the thought. 'Nah, I was just being polite, to be honest. And I'd probably best stay here anyway, just in case any chancers try to sneak in without a ticket.' He pointed through the gate to the camping site in the distance. 'They're up there, mate. Just follow the fuckin' 'orrible smell and you can't go wrong.'

Amit nodded. 'Cheers, Boss. Have a good one.'

He rolled the window up without waiting for a response and drove on through the gate. We sat, stony-faced and silent, until we were a few hundred metres away and Scarface was little more than a dot in the rear-view mirror, then spontaneously celebrated our achievement with wide grins and a high five.

'That was incredible,' I said. 'Your accent was brilliant.'

'I am thinking that I was not so bad myself,' Amit replied. 'Perhaps, when Perry becomes a stand-up comedian, I will endeavour to take Hollywood by storm.'

He drove on a little farther and then pulled up next to the portable toilet cubicles which were lined up like a long row of blue telephone boxes at the periphery of the camping area. We both stepped out of the truck and winced at each other when the rancid smell hit our nostrils a moment later, but we said nothing, preferring instead to get straight on to the job of unstrapping our payload, which was a large plastic portaloo that we had transported horizontally on the pickup box. When the last of the securing straps was loosened, the door of the new toilet opened from the inside and Perry, who was now dressed in black jeans, black boots and a Gorgoroth T-shirt, stood up.

He didn't look particularly happy.

'About frickin' time,' he said. 'Being in there is like being in a coffin.' He sniffed the air and scowled. 'Although, ironically, it smells more like a toilet out here.'

The agent stepped out of the portaloo and hopped off the back of the truck, then stood waiting as we removed our blue overalls to reveal our own festival-friendly outfits. Both myself and Amit wore the same black jeans and boots as Perry, but I was sporting an old-school Slayer T-shirt and Amit had opted for a garment advertising his new-found allegiance to Marilyn Manson.

With all three of us now looking as much like metalheads as it had been possible for us to look after only a brief visit to the nearest shopping center, we started trudging towards the main festival area. Despite our last-minute preparations, I was pleased to see that we actually blended in quite nicely with the genuine visitors, and it was easy for us to quietly tag along with a small group of lads who were heading in the same direction. They were in their late teens or early twenties, and wore black T-shirts with illegible band names scrawled across them in some bizarre white lettering. The smell of stale lager in the air suggested that they'd been drinking rather heavily.

'So did you get anywhere with her, Barry?' one of them asked, rather too casually in my opinion.

'Yeah, mate, but her boyfriend was waiting for her back at the tent, so she only let me cop a feel. Shame, really, 'cos I reckon she would have been well up for it. I'll have to find some other bint to do the honours later.'

And people say that romance is dead.

The festival sounds—by which I mean the roar of an immense crowd of metalheads, the incessant pounding of drums, the squeal of electric guitars and the occasional retch of some bloke throwing up over the shoes of his neighbour (followed by comments like, 'Eww, you 'oribble fucker!')—grew louder as we continued our approach towards the main throng. I didn't know who was currently playing on stage, largely because it wasn't the kind of music that I'd normally listen to, but it seemed to be going down well with the audience and I spotted more than a couple of women showing their appreciation by climbing onto the shoulders of their male friends and promptly flashing their mammaries at the stage. Amit's eyes were on stalks.

'Keep your mind on the job,' Perry said.

'Of course,' Amit replied. 'I am merely observing their rapturous beauty as we go about our business.'

'Believe me, the beauty is only skin deep with people who give it away that easy. It's not worth having.'

Amit shrugged and turned his attention back to navigating a path through the heaving crowd to our intended destination, which was as close as we could possibly get to the right hand side of the main stage. Unfortunately, the main stage seemed to be where everyone else wanted to be too, so squeezing through the masses was becoming more difficult with every step.

It must have taken us half an hour to slowly work our way through the crowd, because the band on stage played at least five ear-shredding songs as we made the journey, and by the time we finally got close to where we wanted to be, my head was throbbing.

Perry said something, but I couldn't make out what it was because of all the noise. Fortunately, he was quick to realise that fact, and chose instead to mime that he wanted me and Amit to stay put whilst he went to scout around the side of the stage. We nodded our understanding and watched as he disappeared into the crowd, and then we did our best to blend in by turning our attention to the stage and pretending to enjoy the music. Two songs later, the agent returned, motioned for us to follow him and turned back the way he'd arrived.

He led us to a marginally less populated area which served as an entrance to a separate part of the venue. This one was marked PRODUCTION STAFF ONLY and was guarded by two big guys who might as well have been twins, because not only were they both dressed head-to-toe in black security uniforms, but they also had shaved heads and thick goatee beards. It was like looking at a night club bouncer after drinking enough to see double.

'I can't be sure,' Perry said, leaning in close enough to make himself heard, 'but they're probably in the production area through there.'

'So we need to get past those two,' I said, nodding sideways at the men in black.

'Yeah. But they're professionals. We won't just be able to bluff our way past them like we did with the attendant at the gate.'

I looked at the two men, with their expressionless faces and huge hands, which I imagined were well used to curling themselves up into equally huge fists. Perry was right. They didn't look like the kind of guys who would be sucked in by some spontaneously concocted reason for why we needed to be allowed into the production area, and now that we were dressed like regular metalheads we couldn't even pretend to be working here in any capacity.

'Are they normal?' I asked.

'I'm pretty sure they're human, if that's what you mean,' Perry said. 'But normal in the general sense?' He looked them up and down again. 'That's a tough one.'

I nodded, reassured that we weren't contemplating going up against demons, at least not at this stage. They were still big blokes, though, and no doubt they were trained in all kinds of Krav-Maga-Tae-Kwon-Do-MMA-Kung-Fu stuff, so the idea of using force to try and get past them was a bit of a non-starter. It was true that there were three of us and only two of them, but Perry was in his fifties, Amit was a vegetarian pacifist and I was averse to hearing the sound of my bones snap in half, so I didn't fancy our chances. On a more positive note, the thought of taking them on physically did give me an alternative idea.

I motioned for Perry and Amit to form a huddle and then I outlined my plan, speaking loud enough for them to hear but not so loud that I would be overheard. 'There's no way all three of us will get past them, so we need to be a bit smarter. You two stage a fight out here, I'll hang back until they come to intervene and then I'll slip into the production area whilst they're distracted.'

'You two fight and I'll go,' Perry said. 'You won't be able to tell which ones are demons and which ones aren't.'

'No offence, mate, but your record on that score was blown at the jazz club.'

Perry didn't appreciate the reminder, but nodded his concession to the fact.

'I do not think that anyone should be fighting at all,' Amit said. 'It is not a good thing for people to be at war with one another. There is already far too much violence in this world for us to be adding to it.'

'No, we're doing this my way,' I said. 'It's my mission and I'm not going to abdicate my responsibility for it. Not again.' I looked at Amit. 'As for the fighting, you were the one who almost broke my nose in the holding cell, remember?'

'But I only punched you because you insisted upon me doing so!' he protested.

'That's right. And now I'm insisting on you doing this. It's only make-belief, so nobody is going to get hurt. Just think of it as more practice for your acting career. Start by picking an argument or something and go from there.'

'Would it be permissible for me to reprieve my accent of the Black Country?' Amit asked.

'You can have whatever accent you like,' I said. 'Just try and make the whole thing as realistic as possible. These guys probably aren't as stupid as they look, and to be honest they don't even look all that stupid, so don't start doing any over-the-top World Wrestling Federation stuff. Capiche?'

Perry gave me an odd look for a moment, and then nodded.

Amit reluctantly followed suit. 'Good luck, my friend. We will be praying hard that Her Divine Gloriousness will see fit to guide your path.'

'You do that,' I said. 'But only if you can pray and fight at the same time.'

CHAPTER TWENTY-FIVE

'What the fuck was that?'

The question had been posed, at high volume and in a flawless West Midlands accent, by Amit to Perry just a minute or two after we had broken our conspiratorial huddle. The two of them had walked a little further away from the PRODUCTION STAFF ONLY area that I was going to attempt to sneak into, whilst I had taken a few steps in the opposite direction so that I could watch the situation unfold from a distance.

'What was what?' Perry asked. He appeared to be genuinely surprised by Amit, probably because he hadn't previously been able to hear the impeccably affected accent from the confines of the portaloo, and maybe also because the would-be Oscar winner had, quite effortlessly, gone from zero to aggro in the space of a heartbeat.

'You know fuckin' well what,' Amit snarled. 'You fuckin' shoved me.'

'I don't know what you're talking about, pal.'

'I'm not your pal, you ignorant twat. I'm pissed.'

'Yeah, well you should probably go back to your tent and sleep it off,' Perry said.

'And who the fuck are you to tell me what to do, old man?'

Perry raised one eyebrow, clearly not appreciating Amit's reference to his age. 'I'm the voice of reason,' he said. 'You should try getting one of your own sometime.'

'You're a fuckin' joke, that's what you are.'

'Oh yeah?'

'Yeah.'

A handful of nearby metalheads had noticed the commotion that was beginning to develop in their vicinity, and had already started stepping away as best they could, given the density of the crowd.

'So, what are you going to do about it?' Perry asked.

'I'll show you exactly what I'm going to do about it, you geriatric bastard.'

And with that, Amit rushed Perry to the ground and the skirmish commenced. Amit was being a lot more aggressive than I had expected, especially in light of his vocal protestations against violence, but Perry adapted to the situation quickly and didn't waste any time in fighting back. Fists were flying, expletives were following, and the two men were soon being cheered on by enthusiastic onlookers.

Within a matter of seconds, Perry and Amit had managed to create an impressive little disturbance. I was careful to distance myself from the crowd that was gathering around them so that I could keep an eye on the guards. They had noticed the argument fairly quickly, but had initially refrained from intervening, probably because they assumed that it was a fuss about nothing and would soon blow over. Now, however, they could see that things were beginning to get out of hand, and they were preparing themselves to do something. One was speaking into a radio and the other was slowly clenching and unclenching his fists.

Eventually, about three minutes after Amit had initiated the confrontation, the two guards abandoned their stations and began forcing their way through the crowd to get to the brawlers at its nucleus. I waited a few moments longer to make sure that they weren't looking back, scanned the area for other staff members—all of whom also seemed to be single-mindedly making their way towards the fight—and then bowed my head and sprinted through the entrance to the production area. I didn't stop sprinting until I was far enough away from the entrance to dip into the shadow of a large truck, pause for breath and think about what I was going to do next.

I looked around. There were fifteen, maybe twenty large vehicles scattered around the compound—a variety of lorries, trucks and tour buses—none of which looked any more significant than the rest. Most were in darkness, but the windows of five or six glowed with light from within, so I figured that those were the likeliest to have people inside them.

After checking over my shoulder to make sure that it was still safe to proceed, I half-crouched, half-ran from vehicle to vehicle, aiming for the nearest one on my shortlist, which just happened to be a large camper van. I slowed down as I got closer to the vehicle and heard the voice of a man talking, followed by the stern response of a woman. The sounds were muffled, and I couldn't see anything through either of the two windows on the side that I had approached because the curtains were closed, so I had no immediate way of knowing whether or not I had struck gold at the first attempt. Creeping around to the opposite side of the van, I saw that the curtains were closed there too, but not quite as well as they should have been, because there was an inch-wide gap to the side of one which I thought would allow me to take a peek inside.

Steeling myself for the task, and checking once again that the coast was clear, I slowly straightened up and looked through the window. What I expected to see, I don't know, but it definitely wasn't a leather-clad woman standing over a heavily tattooed man on all-fours. The man was completely naked, apart from a latex Donald Trump mask which covered his head, and the woman was slapping the man's backside with a flag-shaped paddle bearing the Russian tricolor. The Donald was flinching with every strike.

'You know rules, Donald,' the woman said in a thick Russian accent. 'Niet means niet. Do you understand?'

She gave him a particularly big whack with the paddle, redding his already-glowing butt-cheeks even further.

'Yes, Mistress,' he said breathlessly. 'Thank you, Mistress.'

I watched the scene, wide-eyed and slack-jawed, until the woman reached for a strap-on, at which point I decided that I'd seen quite enough.

The next few semi-illuminated vehicles didn't offer anything of interest. The first two were completely empty, which led me to believe that someone must have left the lights on by mistake, the third was occupied by a small group of blokes playing poker as they swigged from Budweiser bottles and listened to Nirvana, and the fourth was home to a solitary chap who was reading a copy of How to Win Friends and Influence People. Given his preference for reading alone rather than socialising with the thousands of festival-goers who were moshing around just a few hundred feet away, I think I was right to assume that the book was a relatively recent purchase.

By now, all of my hopes were pinned on the last vehicle that was illuminated. It was a sleek, black tour bus which, now that I had seen all of the others, seemed like the one that would most obviously belong to a certain Doran Salt. After glancing around to do my usual check that nobody else was in the area, I took a deep breath to steady my nerves and approached the bus from the side. I listened carefully for signs of life, but there were none. I couldn't see inside either, because there were no windows, so I walked slowly and carefully towards the side door on the driver's side and reached out to open it.

'It's customary to knock before entering.'

Impossibly, the voice was behind me, and I span around to face it, only to confirm what the sickening feeling in my gut had already told me.

That it was him.

Sure enough, Salt was looking down his nose at me, seemingly a foot taller than he had been the last time I'd seen him at the Hell club. Vinnie was standing to his side, smashing the fist of one hand into the palm of the other.

How they had managed to arrive on the scene so suddenly, and seemingly out of thin air, I had no idea. The tour bus was surrounded by plenty of open ground and there really hadn't been a soul to be seen a few moments earlier. That was just a figure of speech, obviously, and I highly doubted that the devil or any of his demons had souls in the theological sense of the word, but I still thought that I should have seen them coming, regardless.

Salt looked around carefully, his eyes scanning the area slowly, before finally turning back to me and raising a brow in mock surprise.

'No bodyguards, Mr Fenton? Don't tell me that they let you come snooping around here without a chaperone.'

I stared him down—or rather, up—and tightened my lips defiantly. My sphincter joined the game a moment later, and without invitation. Perry had warned me that this would be a risky course of action to take, but I had given the middle finger to fear and elected to be brave instead. I wouldn't allow myself to crumble now, even if I was standing face-to-face with the devil himself.

'Incarcerate him,' Salt said, and he watched dispassionately as Vinnie grabbed me by the upper arm, opened the door to the tour bus and bundled me inside. I turned around to protest, but the door had already slammed shut, just inches from my face, and the two bad guys were still on the other side of it.

'Goodnight, Mr Fenton. Sleep well.'

I thought that was a fairly odd thing for the Prince of Darkness to say, but then I heard a hissing sound coming from above, and I suddenly realised what he had meant. Four air vents in the ceiling of the bus, in which I appeared to be the only occupant, were expelling ridiculously thick plumes of a pale white gas, and I was pretty sure that it wasn't someone vaping.

I did my best to avoid inhaling the stuff for as long as possible, first by running around the bus looking for an alternative exit, and then by grabbing a satanic black cushion that was lying around and holding it to my face.

Desperately, I returned to the side door and started banging on it, pulling the pillow away every few seconds to shout for help, but the exercise was futile. Exhausted, I slid down onto the floor and waited for the inevitable wave of sleepiness to overwhelm me.

The problem with being brave, I told myself, is that it can get you into all sorts of trouble.

CHAPTER TWENTY-SIX

A muffled sound seeps, uninvited, into the silent black-ness of my mind and slowly rouses me back to a state of semi-consciousness. I can feel my heart beating, not in my chest, but in the accompanying waves of agony which shoot through my temples every time my most romanti-cally shaped muscle pumps a fresh load of blood through my system. The sensation is unpleasant, but not completely unfamiliar, and it quickly occurs to me that I'm experiencing a hangover of New Year's Day proportions.

So, it's New Year's Day. Except that I can't really remember celebrating New Year's Eve, and although that isn't a particularly uncommon thing, I would normally have at least some memory of the hours leading up to the traditional drunken rendition of Auld Lang Syne. It would usually be the memory of trying to chat up a barmaid in some Irish-themed pub somewhere and failing miserably, but I couldn't even recall going to a pub last night. I defi-nitely went somewhere, though, because I vaguely remember there being loud music. And people. And brawling. And—

And then it all came back in a flood of brightly coloured images. Donington. Little Chef. The portaloo. Perry. Amit. The staged fight. Donald Trump. Finding the tour bus. Turning around and seeing Doran Salt. Being bundled into the bus. Watching the white gas stream in from the air vents in the ceiling...

So, it wasn't a hangover after all. I'd been gassed, and now whatever it was that they had used to knock me out was beginning to wear off, allowing me to regain consciousness and keep a throbbing headache as a souvenir.

I focused again on the sounds that had awoken me from my chemically induced slumber. They were still muffled, but concentrating on them seemed to help make them a little clearer. At first, I thought that the sound was the crashing of waves, and I silently swore at the memory of throwing myself from Brighton Pier, but then I realised that the roar of the ocean was actually the roar of a large crowd of people.

The Ambusti Terrae crowd.

Opening my eyes took some effort, because my heavy eyelids had yet to catch onto the fact that I had indeed regained consciousness and that I now needed to get my arse in gear quickly, but eventually I managed the feat and found myself sprawled out on a hard floor in the middle of a cage. It was a dome-topped cage that I instantly recognised as being exactly like the ones I had seen hanging from the iron rafters of the Hell place. The only difference, apart from the absence of a naked dancer, was that this cage had some kind of heavy covering over it.

Although the covering prevented me from seeing exactly where I was being imprisoned, I knew from the swelling noise of the crowd that it wasn't on the tour bus. I thought that it was more likely backstage somewhere, but there was no music—heavy metal of otherwise—to be heard. The only sound in the air was that of a few thousand metalheads shouting for the sake of shouting, at a steady and rhythmic pace.

No, not shouting.

Chanting.

Doran! Doran! Doran!

As if he were some kind of rock god who they'd all been so keen to see perform live that they would have happily pimped out their grandmothers every weekend for a year in order to buy a ticket.

The chanting continued as I manoeuvred myself into an upright position, paused to allow the renewed pain in my head to subside, and then finally clambered to my feet. I felt more than a little shaky, and I had to hold on to the bars of the cage to steady myself. Quite what they had used to knock me out with, or how long I had spent in a state of ignorant limbo, I had no idea. All I knew was that the gas had packed one hell of a punch, and I could only hope that the after-effects would wear off sooner rather than later, because I still hadn't located the girls, and I doubted that either Perry or Amit would have fared much better.

I had just about gathered myself together when guitars started screeching the introductory riff of Europe's eighties hit, The Final Countdown, at an unnecessarily high volume. Even with my admittedly limited knowledge of heavy metal, it didn't strike me as being the most likely anthem for a satanic rally, but the crowd seemed to love it, having quickly abandoned the chanting in favour of roaring enthusiastically. The tune played for a few bars, and then faded out. A squeal of feedback followed a moment later, at which point, the roaring also died down.

'Well, what a glorious occasion this is.'

The voice, which was hugely amplified by the PA system, was unmistakable. It was the eternally smug voice of Doran Salt addressing his army, but now he sounded even more pleased with himself than he usually did. And who could blame him? I was the only person who had even the slightest chance of preventing him from establishing a new world order, and he had me locked up in a cage like a bloody canary.

'Several days ago,' he continued, 'one man decided that his life was no longer worth living, and so he chose to end it of his own volition by jumping from Brighton Pier into the murky waters beneath. The ocean was only too willing to oblige the man in question, and his pathetic soul was promptly dispatched to the suicide cells of She Who Will Not Be Named.'

I clenched my jaw when I heard him refer to me as a pathetic soul. Who the hell was he to talk? He didn't even have a soul, of any description, pathetic or otherwise, so he really wasn't in any position to judge me on that score.

'Ordinarily, such a soul would have been just as quickly reborn as a lesser being, and it would have mattered little in the grand scheme of things. Fortunately for us, however, the one who jumped was no ordinary mortal, but one who had been foreordained as a key player in a chain of events that would eventually thwart my plan to end the scourge that is mankind, once and for all. His decision to end it all was therefore one that played directly in our favour, because his pitiful suicide automatically set the human race on course for complete and total annihilation, and thereby opened the way for me to fulfil my own destiny as the rightful ruler, not only of this planet, but of all creation.'

My head, although still throbbing, was finally beginning to clear of the fog caused by the gas. I decided that I couldn't just stand there listening to Salt big himself up, so I began looking around the cage, quietly shaking the bars one by one in order to test their integrity. The odds of someone forgetting to lock me in here after going to so much trouble to keep me out of the way were admittedly slim, but I'd have felt like an idiot if I'd neglected to at least check.

'Knowing that her carefully made plan for her beloved human race was well and truly scuppered, She Who Will Not Be Named decided to give the pathetic suicidal soul a second chance. He was returned to Earth in his physical form and was given seventy-two hours to undo the damage that he had inadvertently caused to the cosmic timeline. If he had succeeded in his mission, the timeline would have been restored, humanity—in spite of its myriad shortcomings—would have been redeemed yet again, and our own destiny as the Army of Darkness would have suffered, just as it has always suffered.'

It was no good. Every one of the cage bars that I checked was as strong and secure as I had expected it to be. My prison might have appeared like an oversized birdcage with a tea-towel thrown over the top to keep its occupant quiet, but it was a lot more substantial, and whilst I could hear what was being said over the PA without any problem, there was no way that I was going to be able to escape. I could have rattled the bars, of course, or shouted for someone to get me the hell out, but the only people who could possibly help me were Perry and Amit, and if they had been in a position to do that, they would have done it already. For all I knew, they might well have been sitting in their own cages, listening to the exact same Salt spiel that I was hearing.

'The good news—and I'm referring to the real good news, not the stuff they like to hide in hotel drawers—is that the pathetic soul who is key to the future wellbeing of mankind is just minutes away from failing in his quest, and you have been invited here to witness his spectacular failure in person.'

Did he just say that I was minutes away from failing? Minutes? That meant I must have been out cold for hours.

I felt my heart begin to pound in my chest, as if it too was suddenly feeling desperate to get out of its cage.

'Disciples of the Watch, please feel free to scream, shout, and raise your devil horns high and proud as I present to you the one, the only, and the spectacularly stupid, Mr Gary Fenton.'

At that point, the thick cloth that had been covering my cage was lifted away, and I found myself staring out at a vast ocean of demonic faces. I hadn't been locked away behind the scenes, as I had presumed earlier. Instead, my prison was situated at the front right of the stage, and there was a cloaked-and-hooded guy standing guard next to it. I didn't like the idea, but the hood made him look like an executioner who was just waiting to receive the nod from the man in charge.

The crowd went wild, laughing derisively at the sight of me, imprisoned and impotent to do anything about it.

Salt was standing a few metres away, behind a sleek black pulpit in the middle of the stage. Another few metres beyond that, at the opposite side of the stage, was a second cloaked-and-hooded guard watching over another cage. That second cage was occupied by two people who I recognised instantly.

Natalie and Jenny.

They were looking across at me, their brows furrowed in concern. They didn't look like they had been physically injured, although I couldn't really be sure about that from this distance, but they definitely appeared to be emotionally drained, their puffy red eyes betraying the fact that they had shed more than a few tears in recent hours. Quite what they'd been through since I'd last seen them at Natalie's hotel room on the night of their abduction, I had no idea, but I doubted that it was anything good.

I frowned and shrugged, apologetically. There was no way that such a simple gesture could convey how truly sorry I was to have got them involved in this mess, or to have failed so miserably in doing what God had sent me to do, but I hoped that it might express at least a fraction of my remorse.

'Now I could, of course, simply stand here and tell you all about Mr Fenton's spectacular failure in both life and death,' Salt said when the noise of the crowd had finally died down a little. 'But because he is a product of an age in which reality television and social media reign supreme, I thought that it would be much more fitting to present you with a short YouTube-friendly compilation of his most memorable moments.'

He sneered at me as he turned his attention to the back of the stage, and right on cue the existing backdrop was pulled away to reveal a massive screen. It was much like a screen that you'd see in your local multiplex, but possibly even bigger, and this one was showing a distinctly unflattering image of me standing underneath the SPARE PARTS aisle sign in Piece o' Hut. I was wearing my usual lilac-coloured overalls and scratching my head, my face contorted in an expression of either confusion or imbecility.

It was one of those pictures that you might accidentally take with your phone and delete on the spot. God knows who took it, or when, but the demonic audience quite literally roared with laughter, and I instantly felt my cheeks burn hot with embarrassment.

After a few seconds of that, the lights dimmed, the laughter quietened and the projected image on the big screen gave way to video footage of me walking to work with a miserable look on my face.

'Meet Gary Fenton,' said a male narrator. His voice was deep and booming, as if he were doing the voiceover for the trailer of an action movie. 'He was a man who liked to work hard...'

The video cut to me stacking a display pyramid of boxes in the Piece o' Hut store. When the structure was complete, I turned to walk away from it, but in doing so I accidentally kicked one of the base boxes and brought the whole thing tumbling down behind me.

'To play hard...'

Now the big screen showed me sitting up in the bed of my home in Brighton, reading a Tomb Raider comic. My right hand was hidden under the duvet, but making embarrassingly obvious up and down movements.

'And to die hard...'

The masturbatory scene transitioned to one of me leaping from the side of Brighton Pier in slow motion. My arms and legs were flailing as I plummeted to the ocean beneath.

'And that's when things got really interesting...'

The theme from Mission: Impossible began playing, and the big screen started showing snippets of my life over the last few days: Waking up in the holding cell, being punched by Amit, standing before God and hearing about the damage I had caused, being given my second chance mission, meeting Perry, getting my makeover in London, being coached to act like Cary Grant, getting a book signed by Natalie, being restrained with duct tape by Vinnie, visiting Hell for the first time, dancing with the demon girls in the jazz club, and then trying to fend them off with freshly sliced pieces of fruit...

The shambolic showcase lasted a good ten minutes, and had been put together in such a way that I would be sure to come across as a complete and utter twat. Of course, that had only been possible because I had, in fact, behaved like a complete and utter twat. Even so, seeing my futile attempts to succeed presented one after the other, with absolutely no redeeming points included to counter the negative narrative... Well, let's just say that it wasn't something which made me feel particularly good about myself.

I wondered how Natalie was feeling about the video, and how she had reacted to the revelation that I really wasn't the kind of man I'd attempted to portray. Half-expecting to receive a glare of perfectly well-deserved anger or disappointment, I stole a glance across the stage and was surprised to see her weeping. Jenny was comforting her with quiet words and an arm around her shoulder.

'And so,' the narrator said when the condensed story of my quest to save the world had reached its rather predictable conclusion. 'As Gary Fenton's second chance becomes little more than one more abysmal failure in a lifetime of abysmal failures, the moment of victory for our Army of Darkness draws ever closer.'

The video on the big screen was immediately replaced by the image of a large gothic-style clock face, the like of which you might expect to see in a train station, with ornate black hands and bold Roman numerals. The time was showing as five minutes to midnight, and the second-hand was ticking ominously around the cream-coloured clock-face.

'Yes, indeed,' Salt said as the stage lighting was increased to its previous level. 'In less than five minutes, the deadline by which Mr Fenton must succeed in his quest will be upon us, and the throne will be mine at last.'

The crowd roared once again, and Salt stood behind his pulpit, soaking up the adulation with his arms outstretched and a broad grin on his face.

I looked back at Natalie, who now had her head buried fully in Jenny's embrace, and her distress made me feel worse than I'd ever felt in my entire life. The thought that she could have been mine, and that she would have been if I'd just appreciated my existence a little more, was really depressing, but even more depressing was the fact that I'd actually ruined her life in the process of selfishly trying to end mine.

And now, to top it all, she knew the truth about me. My deception had been revealed by the devil himself, and it had clearly hurt her deeply. I wasn't a Cary Grant type. In fact, I wasn't even a decent Cary Grant impersonator. I was just an extremely average man with a terrible attitude to life who was trapped in a cage and would, in a matter of minutes, be single-handedly responsible for the end of the world.

CHAPTER TWENTY-SEVEN

It's surprising how fluid time can be, and how it always seems to pass at a rate which is inversely proportional to how fast you actually want it to pass. When working at Piece o' Hut on a quiet Tuesday afternoon, five minutes would often feel like a couple of hours, especially if I happened to be on toilet duty. Trying to scrub pensioner skid marks off the ceramic bowl whilst simultaneously holding your breath and turning your head the other way so that you don't have to watch what you're doing is not a lot of fun, believe me.

At other times, five minutes would go by ridiculously quickly. Such as when I used to press the snooze button on my alarm clock in the morning to get a little more rest before my shift, only to have the bloody thing go off again after what felt like just a couple of seconds.

Standing in the cage, I watched the second-hand of the large projected clock sweep past the numbers at an alarmingly brisk pace. There were less than five minutes standing between me and the end of the world, and there was no way for me to prevent it from happening.

I looked out at the crowd, hoping that I might catch an encouraging glimpse of Perry or Amit heading my way, but all I could see were thousands of demons in celebratory mood. What did that mean? Had the agents deserted me? Left me to try and sort things out for myself? No, this mission was theirs as much as it was mine, and leaving me to fail wouldn't be good for them either. So, where were they?

The last time I'd seen the pair, they had been staging the fight just outside the production staff area, and two unamused security guards had left their posts to sort it out. That orchestrated diversion had worked out well from my perspective, because it had allowed me to sneak into the secure area without the guards noticing, but until now I hadn't given any thought to what the consequences might have been for my two friends.

Perry had warned me against my plan, and had suggested going into the secure area instead of me, but I had chosen to ignore his decades of experience and pressed on regardless. I might have thought that I was doing the right thing and acting responsibly, but in retrospect it was pretty clear that I had made the mistake of trying to be a hero, and I'd ended up walking straight into even more trouble.

The minute-hand on the clock ticked forward a notch. It was now four minutes to midnight, and the second-hand continued to move forward at what seemed to be a frighteningly rapid pace.

Salt had described me as a spectacular failure, and I had finally arrived at the point where it was proving impossible for me to continue denying the accuracy of that description. Here I was, a bloke who had failed in both life and death, and now I had failed in my second chance as well.

It was at that point of brutal self-honesty that I did something which I never thought I would do in a million years.

I knelt down in my cage, closed my eyes, and prayed.

Not out loud. Just under my breath. But it was a prayer all the same.

'Please,' I said. 'I don't know whether or not you can hear me, but I'm in trouble. I know that I've fucked up again, and I'm not going to ask you to help me in any way, but if you can do something—anything—to help everyone else, please do it. I don't care what happens to me. But don't let my friends suffer just because I've lived my entire life like a complete jerk.'

It wasn't the most eloquent of prayers, I grant you, and I'm not sure that I honestly believed that it would be heard, but there really wasn't anything else that I could think of doing. This was a desperate situation, and as the old saying goes, desperate times call for desperate measures. Whether or not this particular measure would actually help me in any discernible way... well, I wouldn't have to wait very long to find out.

'Get off your knees.'

For a moment, I wasn't sure if the voice had just been in my head, like some kind of auditory hallucination brought on by stress, or whether someone really had spoken to me. I opened my eyes and looked around, but there was nobody here who hadn't been there a few moments earlier—only Salt, the crowd, and—

The hooded guy guarding my cage.

'Come on, pal. You're no good to anyone down there.'

His voice was muffled, but unmistakable, and the sudden realisation that it was Perry Barr under the hood came as a massive relief. I sprang to my feet without even thinking about it, and I almost grinned at the discovery that I wasn't on my own after all, but then I caught myself before anyone appeared to have noticed, and tried my best to adopt a poker face instead.

'We need to be quick,' I muttered, putting my hand over my mouth and thoughtfully stroking an imaginary moustache so that nobody would see my lips move. Salt eyed me carefully for a long moment, and I feared that my admittedly lame gesture had aroused his suspicions, but then he saw the clock and his customary self-satisfied smile quickly returned. I waited until he had turned back to face the jubilant crowd before risking my follow-up mutter. 'Three minutes left. What's the plan?'

Perry stood motionless as he answered, the mask making it already impossible for anyone to see that he was responding. 'We'll open both cages at two minutes to midnight. When we do, you run across to Natalie.'

'And then?'

'And then you kiss her.'

'I thought that wouldn't count?'

'It probably won't.'

'So what's the point?'

'Better to try and fail than to fail to try.'

Salt shot another fleeting glance in my direction, so I let my hand drop from my face and made an effort to look defeated. It wasn't a difficult thing to achieve. Although I felt much better knowing that Perry and Amit were still on the scene, and I admired their never-say-die attitude, I also knew that the rules were the rules. And the rules made it pretty damn clear that simply snatching a kiss from Natalie wouldn't be enough for me to succeed in my quest. If it would have been, I could have done it days ago, back at the restaurant when everything had seemed to have been going so well.

The second-hand on the clock swept past the six, which meant that both my cage, and the one that imprisoned Natalie and Jenny, would be opened in less than thirty seconds. Figuring that Perry was right, and that trying and failing was a far better way to go that simply standing around like a lemon, I watched the clock carefully and quietly braced myself to make my move.

At exactly two minutes to midnight, Perry Barr sprang into action and unlocked my cage, whilst the guard on the other side of the stage did the same for the girls. Both guards removed their masks, revealing their true identities to Salt and his crowd of demons, and a hiss of surprised hatred filled the arena.

'Seize them!' Salt raged, his face contorting in an expression of wide-eyed lividness.

'Quick, while they're distracted,' Perry said, half-pulling me out of the cage and half-pushing me in Natalie's direction. 'Make it count.'

I nodded and began to run, but I didn't get very far at all before I found myself facing a wall of demons who were hissing and gnashing their teeth. They couldn't touch me, I knew that, but they were doing a perfectly good job of obstructing my path to Natalie.

Surprised that Salt's army had responded so swiftly, I looked back to Perry for a clue, but he was already facing his own problems, having all but disappeared under a mass of writhing assailants. The demons were being as vicious as I'd seen, kicking and punching the agent beneath them in such a way that it was like watching two dozen Vinnie clones unleash their fury at the same time.

Vinnie himself had given Perry quite the beating back in my flat, and if I hadn't stepped in on that occasion it would have been considerably worse, so what chance did the agent have against this angry swarm?

Before I had a chance to answer my own question, a hand rose up from within the pile of demons. It was Perry's hand, and it was holding the glowing ball of Light that I'd seen him use to scare the barman at the Hell club. His attackers quickly scattered to a safe distance, and Perry struggled to his knees. His face was swollen and bloody, and he was breathing hard, but somehow he managed to force a half-smile. 'I think you need this more than I do,' he said, nodding towards the wall of demons in front of me. 'Go get her, pal.'

I wanted to protest, to tell him to wait for me so that we could make our way to the girls together, but he had already thrown the Light towards me, and the demons had been quick to resume their attack. I tore my eyes away from him so that I could concentrate on catching the glowing ball of energy, and by the time I looked back a moment later, he had been engulfed once again by the mass of merciless adversaries.

The Light in my hand was surprisingly cool to the touch. He had intended for me to use it to open up a way to Natalie and snatch a kiss, but could I really let my friend die? I desperately wanted to go back and rescue him—or whatever remained of him—from the demons, but the clock told me that I had less than ninety seconds, and if I did that, there was no guarantee that we'd then get to Natalie in time.

Tightening my lips, I held out the Light and stepped forward towards the wall of demons. It parted like the Red Sea, and on the other side I saw Natalie and Jenny sobbing over the crumpled body of Amit Patel.

He was dead.

Sickened by the sight, I looked back and saw that the demons were pretty close to finishing Perry, too.

A wave of numbness came over me. I don't quite know how long I stood there, looking back and forth at my two friends, one who was already dead and one who was barely alive, but it felt like an eternity. I had only known Perry and Amit for a few days, but they were probably the best friends I ever had.

'Sixty seconds, Mr Fenton,' Salt boomed over the PA system. 'I think it's safe to say that your time is up.'

Ignoring his voice, I took a few more steps towards Natalie. She looked up at me, her eyes all wet, red and puffy. I had expected to see them full of anger, disappointment or maybe even hatred, but all I saw was tenderness, compassion, and a heartbreaking glimpse of what might have been.

Swallowing back the hard lump that had somehow lodged itself in the back of my throat, I knelt down beside Natalie. I took her right hand in mine, and held the Light aloft in my left to continue keeping the demons at bay.

'I am so sorry,' I told her. 'I wish I had time to explain, but I don't. Just believe me when I tell you that I love you. But Perry and Amit are my friends too, and if I don't do what I'm about to do, I'll never be able to forgive myself.'

Without waiting for a response, I stood up and headed back towards the mass of demons who were attacking Perry. They dispersed as soon as they sensed the Light, leaving behind a very-nearly-dead former salesman of the North Carolina Brush Company.

'Hey,' he said, doing his best to grin through swollen, bloodied lips. 'Did we win?'

I knelt down beside him, glanced at the clock and frowned. 'If you mean did I get the girl, then no. And with less than thirty seconds left, I don't think that's going to happen.'

'Then why d'you come back to me here?' he asked. 'The whole of mankind is depending on you, pal.'

'I know,' I said. 'But I suddenly realised, we're only in this situation because I existed in the first place. Getting the girl and correcting the timeline has been the only solution we've pursued, but there's another one. It's been there all along.'

Standing up once again, I walked over to the pulpit, which Salt was now using as a shield between himself and the approaching Light in my left hand, and I grabbed him by the collar. The crowd fell silent, as if stunned that a pathetic mortal soul—albeit one bearing the Light—could apprehend their Dark Lord so easily.

'No, pal,' Perry said, clearly understanding what I intended to do.

'I'm not afraid any more, Perry,' I said. 'If there was another way, I'd take it, because I'm really not feeling suicidal any more. But there's no time to do anything different. You and Amit, Natalie and Jenny... you're the only friends I ever had. And I'd rather make things right once and for all than let you all down yet again. I need to win this time.'

'I know,' he said. 'But not like that.'

'Thanks for everything, Perry,' I said. 'And say hi to Rita for me.'

A final glance at the clock told me that there were five seconds left.

I looked over at Natalie and mimed a kiss. 'I love you.'

'Oh, please,' Salt groaned.

'And you, Mr Salt... You're coming with me.'

And with that, I slammed the Light squarely into my chest and tore my soul apart into a quadrillion little pieces.

CHAPTER TWENTY-EIGHT

Having your soul torn apart into a quadrillion little pieces might sound quite painful, but I didn't feel a thing. There was an explosion of sorts, and an instant later my consciousness seemed to be expanding in all directions at once. First, it filled the Donington area, then the whole of England, then the whole of Europe, then the whole world, then the solar system, and then I didn't have a bloody clue where I was, because it felt like I was everywhere and nowhere at the same time. There was a sense of continued expansion at an impossible rate, but also of complete and utter stillness.

Like the Big Bang personified, I had started as a singularity, and the introduction of a quantum fluctuation (the slamming of the Light into my chest) had triggered my rapid inflation. Don't ask me how I knew that, but I knew it with the same kind of certainty that I knew two plus two made four.

My expansion continued at breakneck speed for what

I perceived to be a minute or two, until it felt as if my consciousness had filled the entire universe.

And then it stopped.

For a split second there, I experienced an indescribable moment of complete clarity. Clarity about what? About life, the universe, and everything. For that briefest of moments, absolutely everything made perfect sense to me. Birth, death, love, hate, calm, stress, health, sickness, excitement, boredom, faith, fear, energy, apathy, gain, loss —we tend to think of these things as being polar opposites, but now I realised that they really weren't. They were all parts of the exact same thing, like the many aspects of a single diamond, and all of them had a role to play in keeping the whole in a state of perfect balance. A similar principle applied to human beings. We all like to imagine that we're completely separate people, as unique and special as individual snowflakes, but from this expanded perspective I saw that there was no real separation at all. Instead, we were like the many leaves on a single oak tree, which have a semblance of being separate from each other, but which are in fact connected, like varied expressions of a single organism.

Then, as soon as I had become aware of all this, my consciousness started contracting just as rapidly as it had expanded. Like a balloon that had been inflated, almost to the point of bursting, and then released, my awareness quickly snapped back to its initial state of singularity.

Having been one with everything, I was now back to being just one.

'Welcome back.'

It was the voice of God.

We were back in the same corporate-style board room

that I had been escorted to from the holding cell a few days earlier, and just like before, we were sitting at opposite ends of the conference table. This time, however, God wasn't staring me down or flaring her nostrils at me in blatant disapproval. On the contrary, she was smiling broadly, and her friendly expression suddenly made her seem like the warmest being in the universe.

Given that I hadn't exactly achieved what I'd been commissioned to achieve, it was a smile that made me deeply suspicious. And why was I still here in the first place? I'd only used the Light on myself in order to erase myself from existence, and hopefully put things right in the process so that the people I cared about could go back to living their lives as usual.

'What happened?' I asked. 'I thought the Light would annihilate me?'

'You were right. It would.'

'So how come I'm still here?'

God didn't respond immediately, but instead rose from her seat and swept her hand through the air. As if by magic—if you can accurately describe anything that God does as magic—a huge array of blank video screens appeared on the wall to my left. The wall, which had a holographic quality, was probably fifty screens wide and thirty screens deep.

'Most people believe that there is just one universe' she said. 'But that isn't the case at all. Every choice that a human being makes, regardless of whether it is large or small, wise or foolish, effectively creates a brand new universe for them to occupy from that point on, until the next time they make a decision.'

She waved her arm again and the wall of screens came

to life. Each screen was displaying a different scene, like a bank of video surveillance monitors.

'These are just a handful of the billions of universes that you have personally created up to this point,' she told me.

I looked closer at the screens, and was surprised to see that I really was featured on all of them. On the first screen, I was working at Piece o' Hut, but I was wearing a suit and tie instead of the usual lilac uniform.

'That's the universe which you created when you made the decision to take your job seriously instead of complaining about it,' God said. 'You were promoted three times in the first year, you took over as the Brighton store manager in the second, and you were made the regional manager three years after that.'

I stared at the screen. It was weird, seeing myself looking so responsible, but I actually appeared to be quite happy as I went about doing my work, which was an even stranger concept for me to get my head around.

'On the next screen you'll see the universe that you created when you decided that crime was a better career choice than any kind of gainful employment.'

She indicated the monitor, which displayed me sitting on a bunk in a prison cell. I was looking rather wistfully at a picture of Brighton Pier that I'd stuck to the wall with tape. The irony of that scenario wasn't lost on me.

'And so it goes on,' God said. 'Each screen represents a different decision you made which effectively took you into a different universe of your own creation.'

I scanned the bank of screens carefully, and was amazed by the variety of situations they portrayed. In one universe I was homeless, and in a second I ran a soup kitchen. In a third universe I had been arrested and charged for driving under the influence of alcohol, and in a fourth I was an ambulance driver. In a fifth universe I was the drummer in a jazz band called the Gary Fenton Five. Other universes had me married, divorced, with kids, without kids, overweight, incredibly healthy, happy, sad, intelligent, stupid, popular, disliked... the diverse range of lives that I had lived, or rather, that I was currently living in alternate realities, was mind-blowing.

It was then that I noticed a solitary blank screen in the bottom right corner of the video wall.

'Why isn't that screen showing anything?' I asked.

'That was where you made the decision to use the Light on yourself,' she answered, 'which effectively erased you from existence.' She looked at me carefully. 'Why exactly did you do that, by the way?'

I thought back to the moment before I had slammed the Light into my chest, when all I had cared about was putting things right for my friends.

'Because I figured, if I'd never existed, I'd never have won your cosmic lottery, and I'd never have been able to mess everything up in the first place.'

'But you surely realised that someone else would have then been assigned to fulfil the same role.'

'To be Natalie's soul mate, have children with her and eventually have a great grandson who would save the human race, you mean?' I swallowed hard, trying not to think too much about the idea of her being with someone else for the rest of her life instead of me. 'Yeah, I realised that. But I'd rather Natalie be happy without me than have her life ruined because of me.'

God nodded.

'Besides,' I continued, 'there was no way that I'd have been able to finish the quest in the way you'd asked me to, so taking myself out of the equation was the only option. What I don't understand is how I can still be here talking to you when I shouldn't even exist.'

'Well, that isn't all down to you.' She waved her arm through the air for a third time and the bank of video screens merged into one giant display. 'Watch.'

The display showed me standing on the stage at Donington with the Light in my hand. I was ready to grab Doran Salt, and I glanced at the clock behind me, which revealed that it was just five seconds before midnight. Then I looked over at Natalie, mimed a kiss and told her, 'I love you.'

'Oh, please,' Salt groaned.

The on-screen Gary Fenton tightened his grip on Salt's collar.

'And you, Mr Salt... You're coming with me.'

And then, exactly as I remembered, I watched myself slam the Light into my chest. There was a colossal explosion, with energy radiating so bright that the screen turned completely white for a second or two. When the light had faded and the image of the scene had returned, I saw that I had vanished, and so had Salt.

God pointed at the screen and the movie paused. She looked at me, expectantly. 'Does that answer your question?'

I looked at her, and then back at the freeze-frame image on the screen, but I couldn't for the life of me figure out what she was talking about. 'No, not really,' I answered. 'Like I said, I used the Light to annihilate myself, and yet I'm still here. It doesn't make any sense at all.'

The large woman sighed. It was the kind of response that a mother with infinite patience might give to a clueless son who couldn't seem to grasp the difference between up and down, which I thought was a bit rich, given that her video explanation hadn't told me anything that I wasn't already aware of.

'Alright,' she said. 'Let's look again, shall we?' She flicked her index finger to the left and the video rewound to the beginning. 'Now watch more closely.'

The video started playing and once again the screen showed me standing in the middle of the stage with the Light in my hand. He looked at the clock behind him, then at Natalie, mimed a kiss and said, 'I love you.'

'Oh, please,' Salt groaned.

The on-screen Gary tightened his grip on Salt's collar.

'And you, Mr Salt... You're coming with me.'

God paused the film at that point.

'Now take a good look at what you see,' she said.

I stared at the scene. Perry was on the floor and seemed to be protesting. Salt was wide-eyed with shock at the prospect of being taken down by a pathetic soul such as me. I was looking pretty damn determined, even if I do say so myself. And over on the other side of the stage, the girls were—

'Oh my God.'

Natalie was blowing a kiss back at me.

'You're welcome,' God said. 'Now keep watching.'

The scene resumed playing in slow motion, and I saw Natalie mouth the words, 'I love you too,' barely a fraction of a second before the Light hit my chest and the explosion turned the screen white.

I stood, stunned, as God turned off the screen with another wave of her arm.

'She said she loved me,' I said, hardly able to believe my own words. 'But why? I only had one meal with her.'

'In person, yes. But it was enough to give her an inkling that you were someone special. And Salt's final attempt to humiliate you with his video montage showed her the lengths you had gone to for her, warts and all, and that was enough for her to recognise you as her soul mate. Then, when you proclaimed your feelings towards her at the very end, she instinctively made a profession of her own love for you and she sealed it with a heartfelt kiss.'

'Not on the lips, though.'

'When you really love someone, the connection goes far beyond the physical,' God told me. 'Which means that, despite odds which Moses himself would have balked at, you finally managed to succeed in your quest after all.'

I looked at her, trying hard to process everything that she was telling me. It was a lot to take on board, and a part of me felt like it was almost too good to be true. 'So the universe is safe? The one that I almost fucked up royally?'

She nodded with a smile. 'Your quest was successful, the timeline has been restored, mankind has a long future ahead of it and in return you now get to enjoy your second chance at life.'

'With Natalie?' I asked, hopefully.

'Of course.'

I nodded appreciatively, finally allowing the good news to sink in, but as I ruminated over our conversation of the last few minutes, I realised that I still had one or two unanswered questions.

'What about the blank screen that was in the corner? You said I'd annihilated myself and erased myself from existence.'

'And so you did, because in that particular universe you didn't think to express how you felt about your soul mate and so you gave her nothing to respond to. Sometimes it's the tiniest of decisions which make all the difference between ultimate success and complete and utter failure.'

I nodded. This was beginning to make sense, because it all seemed to boil down to cause and effect. Every decision that I had ever taken had created a slightly different —or sometimes, a completely different—universe, and that one decision to tell Natalie that I loved her had quite literally saved the day.

'What about Perry and Amit?' I asked.

Another wave of her arm brought the big screen back to life, and I saw that Perry was laughing and joking with a gorgeous looking woman.

'Is that Rita?' I asked.

'Yes,' God said. 'Perry is back in the fifties with his own soul mate, and they will now enjoy a long and happy life together, exactly as I originally intended. His old friend Lola has been well taken care of too, you'll be pleased to hear.'

I nodded my appreciation. 'And Amit?'

The screen flicked to a different scene, where Amit was standing on a tropical beach taking glamour shots of nude models.

'He's still quite the pervert, I'm afraid.' She looked at

me and smiled. 'But at least he's a happy and productive one.'

I grinned at her comment, which seemed as ungodly as any that I might have made in the same situation.

'You know, if you ended all suffering then people would be happy like that all the time.'

God shrugged. 'Perhaps. But every human being is really the god of his or her own universe. I'm not into micromanagement, and sometimes shit happens. The important thing isn't what happens to a person in life, but how they choose to handle it. A professional poker player can be dealt the worst possible hand and still win the pot. It's all a question of attitude and being willing to play the game to the very best of your ability.'

Her words made a lot of sense. Life wasn't about being dealt the perfect hand, or being born with a silver spoon in your mouth. It was more about how you played whatever cards you were dealt, and being willing to make the best out of whatever situation you might find yourself in.

'So, Mr Fenton,' she said. 'Are you willing to play the game?'

I looked at her. She had a glow of kindness and compassion about her that I honestly hadn't seen on previous occasions. That was probably because I hadn't been ready or willing to see it, but now I was more than ready, and her wholly benevolent nature was as clear to me as the smile on her face.

'Yes,' I said. 'I'm willing. And I'm sorry, for not believing in you.'

'Like I told you before, I don't give a flying fuck if you believe in me or not,' she said. 'The only thing that matters is that you believe in yourself.'

CHAPTER TWENTY-NINE

Life is sometimes a pain in the arse.

Not just for people who consider themselves unlucky, but for everyone.

It doesn't matter who you are. At some point, shit happens.

It might be something relatively small, like stubbing your toe as you climb into bed, burning the dinner, or remembering at breakfast time that you ran out of coffee the day before. Or, it might be something more serious, such as failing an exam, losing your job after giving twenty years of service, being dumped by your partner, or being diagnosed with an illness that won't go away.

The details are irrelevant, because it isn't what happens to you that colours your life, or makes you happy, or sad. It's how you choose to respond to what happens to you.

In every moment, no matter where you find yourself, you have the opportunity to make a brand new decision that will change the course of your life. If you lose your job, you can wallow in self-pity or you can decide to take fate in your own hands and determine to find an even better one. If your partner runs off with someone else, you can either cry about it or you can say good riddance and set out to find someone more deserving of your affections. If you're diagnosed with an illness that won't go away, you can either feel sorry for yourself or you can choose to be an inspiring example to others by facing it head-on with strength and courage.

It isn't always easy to choose a positive response, but life isn't meant to be easy. Life is a game, and like all good games, it can be challenging at times. If you realise this, you can actually learn to embrace the challenges, and set out to become a modern-day alchemist who turns problems into opportunities.

Take my game, for example.

My name is Gary Fenton. I'm thirty-five years old and I live on my own in a small flat in a not-so-desirable part of Brighton. The place needs work, but I'm lucky enough to have a job in a local DIY store that gives me a generous staff discount, and so I'm currently renovating it myself, albeit at a snail's pace. My landlord is more than happy that I'm improving his property, and to show his appreciation he's promised not to increase my rent for the duration of my tenancy, no matter how long I stay, so we both win.

As far as relationships are concerned, well... there haven't been any serious ones since I was in my late twenties. I could get miserable about that, but there's some part of me that believes in fate, or destiny, and so I just relax and trust that the right person will come along at the right time. Of course, she's unlikely to just fall from the sky like an angel, which is why I try to stack the odds in my favour by sprucing myself up and taking a walk along the busy Brighton seafront every Friday night. I'm heading out tonight, as a matter of fact, because it's Friday the thirteenth, and superstitious people say that it's lucky for some, so why not for me?

I started getting ready for my weekly walk towards Brighton Pier at just before eight o'clock in the evening. I'd already shaved and showered, and I was just putting my jacket on when the doorbell rang. I don't usually get visitors, especially in the evenings, so when I opened the door I half-expected to see a pizza delivery guy in need of directions. But that wasn't the case.

The caller was a woman, and she was gorgeous.

'Thank God,' she said. 'This is the fifth door that I've tried and you're the first person to answer.'

'I was just heading out myself, to be honest,' I said. 'Are you looking for someone in particular?'

'No, not really. It's just that, well, my car's broken down, and my mobile seems to have died for no reason. I was hoping… do you have a phone that I could use, by any chance?'

'Of course,' I said, and I stepped to one side to clear the way for her to enter. 'Come on in.'

'Perfect,' she smiled. 'Thank you.'

She stepped into the hall and then she paused, looked at me carefully and cocked her head to one side.

'I don't know why, but you look strangely familiar to me. Have we met before?'

'No,' I said. 'I don't think I've had that pleasure before. My name is Gary.'

She smiled again. 'Well, I'm very pleased to meet you, Gary. I'm Natalie.'

We shook hands, and the moment the skin of my palm touched hers, I swear on all things holy that something special happened. It sounds corny, I know, but I suddenly felt more alive than at any other time in my life. I don't think that the experience was mine alone, either, because her eyes widened, looking like perfect pools of baby blue that made me want to jump into them and splash around for the rest of my days. She was still smiling, too, and it was the most gorgeous smile I'd ever seen, with the most kissable lips imaginable.

'Wow,' I said.

'Yeah,' she agreed.

And all of a sudden, I knew—don't ask me why or how, I just knew—that my game was never going to be the same again.

ABOUT THE AUTHOR

Mark Eldish is a professional writer whose irreverent and often disruptive sense of humour have made him largely unemployable in any regular office environment.

After spending two decades working as a freelance writer for publishing and media companies around the world, he eventually saw the light and became a novelist.

Mark currently lives in Britain with his family. In his spare time he likes to laugh at his own jokes.

You can find out more about Mark Eldish at his website: www.markeldish.com, or connect with him personally on Twitter @eldish_mark.